FOREVER IN LOVE

A Walker Island Romance, Book 5

Lucy Kevin

FOREVER IN LOVE
A Walker Island Romance, Book 5

During the past year, Emily Walker has been thrilled to watch each of her sisters fall in love one after the other. Having stepped into her late mother's shoes nearly two decades ago, Emily has always put her family first. A family that also includes Michael Bennet. Tall, strong, and good with his hands, he moved in as a teenager after the tragic deaths of his parents. But while the rest of her sisters look at Michael like a brother, Emily has always had to fight against seeing him as something more. So much more...

Michael owns the island's top construction company, but he's never too busy to help out at the rambling Walker house whenever one of the women needs him to pitch in. Especially Emily, the Walker sister he's had a major crush on since the day he first set eyes on her. The time was never right to turn their friendship into anything more, but after so many years of unrequited love, he can't hold back his feelings anymore.

When Michael surprises Emily at her sister's wedding with his declaration of love, suddenly she can't help but wonder if her best friend was actually more all along. Maybe even her one true love that will last forever...

CHAPTER ONE

Spring fever was rampant on Walker Island—from the cherry blossoms to the births of the lambs to the antsy students who couldn't concentrate on anything but their upcoming break. But the best thing of all about this spring was the fact that Emily Walker's sister, Morgan, was only moments away from walking up the aisle to marry her longtime love, Brian Russell.

For the past few weeks, Emily had been simultaneously trying to manage her small horde of students in her job as high school counselor *and* working to make sure every detail of her sister's wedding would be perfect. Morgan had assured her several times that she didn't have to help with each little thing connected with the wedding. And Emily knew Morgan had access to a legion of film people who were experts on everything from photography to catering. But this was her sister's *wedding,* and nothing was more important to Emily than taking care of her family. She wanted to take the time to look for the perfect string quartet, the best caterer, and the most talented florist, even if those were all things the wedding planner could have taken care of.

Morgan and Brian had chosen to hold the wedding at the old Walker family homestead, surrounded by wild flowers and berries, cherry blossoms, and a stunning carpet of meadow grass. The florist had decorated the chairs with herb bouquets using the same plants that Morgan worked with for her exclusive cosmetic line. A gorgeous flower and herb covered arch stood at the end of the garden where the ceremony would take place. The string quartet played a selection of music with a springtime theme as they waited for the cue to begin the processional, and the open, natural space was the perfect counterpoint to the elegant music and the beautifully dressed guests.

All the Walker sisters were bridesmaids, wearing lavender dresses, but Emily's youngest sister, Hanna, was the only one who had lavender streaks in her blond hair to match. Hanna's husband, Joel Peterson, was waiting in the crowd of friends and family. He looked a little windblown, as if he had just stepped off a boat that morning, which Emily figured he probably had. A sixty-year feud between the Walkers and the Petersons had finally come to an end when Hanna and Joel had fallen in love. Fortunately, the Petersons all seemed to have adjusted well to the idea of having Hanna Walker in the family.

Paige, Emily's second-oldest sister, was clearly wishing she could dance to the music the string quartet was playing. Paige's boyfriend, TV and movie star Christian Greer, was sitting in the front row next to their grandmother, Ava. Paige and Christian had flown in two days ago from the set of his latest movie to be here for the wedding, and Emily couldn't wait to see them dance together again. They really were the most unexpectedly perfect couple.

Rachel, who was closest in age to Emily, looked as fit and lean as Paige these days, thanks to a life spent adventuring around the world with Nicholas, the professional surfer she'd fallen in love with. Rachel's six year old daughter, Charlotte, stood between Emily and Rachel in her own miniature bridesmaid's dress. Emily marveled at how much taller her niece had grown since she'd last seen Charlotte at Christmas.

Emily was thrilled to have everyone together again. Her mother, Ellen, would have absolutely loved to know that Morgan was getting married to the boy she'd loved ever since her sister was a teenager. When Rachel reached for her hand and gave it a squeeze, Emily knew her sister was thinking about their late mother, too. On days like this, Emily couldn't shake the feeling that their mother was watching over all of them...and that thought made everything so much better.

"Here she comes," Hanna whispered excitedly as Morgan's limousine pulled up to the edge of the gravel road leading to the meadow. "I wish she had let me film this."

"Morgan wanted you to be a part of the bridal party today," Emily whispered back. "Besides, there are already enough cameras here to film a full-length movie."

Morgan got out of the limo, and the photographers all jostled for position. With their father by her side and the wedding planner making final adjustments to her gown, the photographers were having a field day trying to capture every angle imaginable. Morgan was a well-known name thanks to her TV makeover show, and she attracted attention wherever she went. The fact that she was getting married to her childhood sweetheart had put the entertainment news programs into overdrive.

Morgan and Brian's guest list included not only the likes of Christian Greer and Nicholas Quinn, but also half a dozen of Morgan's celebrity clients with whom her sister was close. But no matter how good-looking the guests were, Morgan outshone them all. In her stunning white gown, she looked the way brides only ever seemed to look in the movies—so perfect that Emily almost found it hard to believe it was her little sister and not a movie star.

Emily teared up as Morgan moved up the aisle on the arm of their father. Her sister's eyes were full of love and happiness as she gazed in wonder at her groom. And from Brian's awestruck expression, it was obvious that he couldn't wait to pledge himself to Morgan forever.

Today felt like a wonderful moment of completion. Emily had spent so much of her life looking after her four younger sisters, stepping in to take over when their mother died twenty years ago. Their father had been so devastated by the loss of his beloved wife that he hadn't known how to cope with being left to raise five girls without his wife by his side. They'd all grown up in Grams' big old home, and Ava Walker had always been there for them. Being a nurturing type, Emily had stepped into her mother's shoes as much as she could by cooking meals, taking her sisters to school, and helping them out with advice about boys.

All she'd ever wanted was for her sisters to be happy. Knowing that each of them had found true love meant everything to her. Morgan and Brian had always been meant to be, even if their road to true love had been a little bumpy. Get Paige and Christian dancing together and it was like there was no one else in the world. Rachel, Nicholas, and Charlotte had formed their own perfect little traveling family. And Hanna and Joel only had eyes for each other.

What's more, each of her sisters had made so much of their professional lives. Hanna was pursuing the film career she'd always dreamed of. Rachel was finally living the adventures she longed for. Paige was choreographing special projects and even dancing on stage. And Morgan's TV show was drawing in bigger and bigger numbers every week it aired.

Emily looked up at the bright blue sky and thought, *I hope I did a good job filling in for you, Mom.*

"Why are you crying, Aunt Emily?" Charlotte whispered.

Emily ran a hand over her niece's hair as she bent down to whisper back, "Because I'm so happy."

"Then shouldn't you be smiling?"

"Sometimes," Emily told her as she smiled through her tears, "when I'm really happy, I cry and smile all at the same time."

"We're here today to celebrate the marriage of Morgan and Brian..."

Everything was absolutely perfect as the bride and groom stood hand-in-hand about to say the vows they'd written for each other.

"Brian," Morgan said in a clear, sweet voice as she turned to face her groom, "I've loved you since we were kids. I let life come between us for far too long, but I never stopped loving you. And coming back to you was the best decision I've ever made. However tangled up the garden of my life gets, I'll always love you. Forever and ever."

"Morgan..." Brian had to stop when he got choked up, and Emily knew every last one of the wedding guests got choked up right along with him. "I've loved you for as long as I can remember. I'll never stop loving you, and I'll never stop telling you how much I love you. Wherever life leads us, I'll be right here at your side every single step of the way."

A short while later, after Morgan and Brian slipped platinum wedding bands on each other's fingers and kissed to seal their vows, Emily applauded with everyone else as the radiantly happy husband and wife walked down the aisle with their arms tight around each other. Emily smiled at her best friend, Michael Bennet, who was Brian's best man. Michael was moving toward her to begin their own walk back down the aisle behind the happily wed bride and groom, when she caught his expression...and stumbled in her heels.

Because Michael wasn't looking at her as if she was simply his friend. Instead, she was stunned to realize that he was gazing at her in the same way that Brian had been looking at Morgan as she'd walked up the aisle on their father's arm.

As if she was his *forever.*

* * *

Once the reception got started and the first champagne toast had been offered, Emily took a few minutes to visit the ladies room and check her makeup. She knew all those happy tears must have done some damage. But as she gazed at herself in the mirror, she was pleased to see she still looked good—she'd had her long blond hair done up in a loose French twist, and the hairstyle showed off the gorgeous chandelier earrings Morgan had given her as a bridesmaid's gift. She had chosen to have her dress made in a sheath style, and it showed off her curves in a way that Morgan had approved of wholeheartedly. *You need to dress like that more often,* had been her sister's exact words.

But if Emily secretly hoped that someday someone would say she was beautiful and sweep *her* off her feet...well, she'd certainly never admitted it anyone. Not even, most of the time, to herself.

It was just that this wedding had been so incredibly romantic. That had to explain why Michael had looked at her like that—as if being friends was only the beginning for them.

She decided that she couldn't fault him for being just as swept away by all of it as she had been. And if there was an even more secret part of her that wished the longing on Michael's face when he'd taken her hand in his to walk down the aisle had actually been real...

No. She couldn't let herself go there. Not now.

Not *ever.*

"Never mind your daydreams, Emily Walker," she said as she looked into the mirror, "you've got a wedding to supervise."

Emily walked back outside determined to check with the wedding planner to see if anyone needed help with anything. Every moment of her sister's big day needed to be perfect, and she would be the one to ensure that happened.

Thankfully, so far everything was going really well. Brian and Morgan were greeting their guests with enthusiasm. Paige and Christian were sharing a quiet moment over a glass of champagne, so gorgeous they looked as if they should be on the cover of a magazine. Hanna and Joel were talking to one of the producers who had come to the wedding. Nicholas and Rachel were making sure Charlotte had a good time even though there weren't many other kids at the wedding. And Emily could see their grandmother, Ava, off to one side, effortlessly charming some Hollywood types.

"Canapés," Emily said to herself, as she realized one of the many food stations was looking a little picked over. "We need more canapés." She'd set off through the crowd of guests in search of the caterer when a familiar voice caught her attention.

"There you are. You look as if you're working instead of partying."

Emily spun around at the sound of Michael's voice. She had to admit he looked good in a suit. Actually, he looked *amazing*. He was clean-shaven and wearing a light cologne that was subtle, but really nice. His dark eyes and dark hair stood out against his close shave, and the muscles he'd built up working construction certainly filled out his suit nicely.

"You look gorgeous, Emily."

"Thank you." She tried not to blush. After all, this was *Michael.* He'd practically lived at the Walker house since they were both teenagers. "You clean up pretty nicely yourself."

He smiled, and her heart went pitter-patter in

her chest despite all her warnings to herself not to let it happen. "Can you take a break for a few minutes? I'd like to show you something."

If it had been anyone but Michael, she might have said no so that she could keep an eye on every moment of the wedding reception. But he was her best friend. When his parents passed away, he had moved in with her family. One way or another, he had been at the house virtually every day since. Now that he was older, he lived in his parents' old house on the other end of the street from hers, but he still helped out the family whenever they needed him.

"Okay," she agreed, "but we need to make this quick. I want everything to be perfect for Morgan."

Michael glanced over to where Morgan was dancing cheek to cheek with Brian. "I think a meteorite could strike the island right now and she wouldn't notice."

"I know, which is why I've got to keep an eye on everything—to make sure that she doesn't *have* to worry about any of it."

Michael shook his head. "You are incorrigible." But he was smiling as he said it. "Just come with me without arguing for once."

"Now where would the fun be in that?" Emily countered, although today she felt less playful and more nervous as she teased him back.

She'd always found him fun and sweet—and extremely attractive—but those were only more reasons why she'd been so careful over the years to make sure they remained friends without ever crossing over into something more. Michael was a *very* important part of their family, and Emily would never let her own secret longings risk ruining that.

She let Michael lead her away from the party, through the back forty and up toward a low rise that overlooked the whole affair. "You know I'm not wearing shoes for hiking, right?"

Michael smiled again. "Don't worry, if your feet start bothering you, I'll pick you up and carry you. Just like that time in high school when we were hiking and you twisted your ankle on the trail."

Again, she worked to ignore the little flutter in her belly at the memory of Michael's hands on her—and the thought of him holding her again like that today. But she couldn't keep her heart from beating just a little faster as they continued walking, and as much as she wanted to blame her racing pulse on the hill, today she couldn't quite get herself to believe it.

Emily had known Michael long enough to know when he had something on his mind, something he wanted to say to her. And the thought of what that might be sent butterflies tumbling around in her stomach.

The view from the top of the rise was spectacular. They could see all the way to the inlet, but their attention was drawn to the wedding below. All their friends and family were there, her sisters dancing with the men they loved while Grams was waltzing around the dance floor with another guest.

"Why did you bring me up here, Michael?"

He let his hand linger on her arm. "Because you've been running around all day, all week, all month, trying to take care of every last detail, and I wanted to make sure you took a moment to stop and see all this. I wanted you to see your family. To see how happy they all are. To see how well all your sisters turned out. Everything *is* perfect, Emily."

"The wedding planner has done a really good job."

His smile was warm, so warm that she swore she could feel the heat from it moving over her skin. "I know how much work you put into this wedding. How much heart and soul, too. Making something like this look effortless and relaxed takes a lot of work and planning. But I'm not just talking about the wedding. You've done a great job making sure everyone is happy and well-loved." He took her hands in his and tugged her gently toward him so that she was looking directly in his eyes as he said, "And now it's your turn."

CHAPTER TWO

Michael had been in love with Emily his entire life. After all these years, he knew her different expressions—the way she lit up whenever her sisters had good news to share, the way she couldn't stop frowning when she was worried about them, and how much genuine caring there was in her eyes every time she counseled a student at the high school or was helping out with one of the many island community projects.

Today, however, he couldn't quite figure out what she was thinking as she said, "What do you mean, it's my turn now?"

All the Walker sisters had the same blond hair, blue eyes and high cheekbones—the extraordinary good looks they'd inherited from their grandmother. Yet it had always been Emily Michael had been drawn to, with her effortless grace, her self-assured manner, her kind and caring nature...and her sexy girl-next-door appearance.

The strains from the string quartet drifted up to where they stood, and twilight was settling in over the scene. It did look magical, and it was not hard to see that the guests were having a great time.

But Michael only had eyes for Emily.

Always Emily.

He knew how much she had put into helping raise her sisters up and making sure things didn't fall apart after their mother died. Which was why he'd forced himself to wait to have this moment with Emily until she could stop focusing on her sisters' lives and finally think about her own.

"You did an amazing job bringing up your sisters," Michael replied. "And when you aren't working at the school, you're always getting involved in local projects."

"I like my job and working with the community. And I like looking after my sisters, too." Her mouth quirked up slightly at the corner as she added, "Someone has to."

He gestured to the scene below them, where her sisters were all dancing. "Like I said, you did great with your sisters, but they're all more than capable of looking after themselves. They finally all have the lives they've always wanted. They're with men they love." He didn't take his eyes off of her face as he said, "I know as well as anyone that you've been putting off your own happiness to make sure that everything works out for them.

And now, maybe it's time to think about what *you* want for once."

She was frowning as she turned her beautiful blue eyes to him again, and just like always, he immediately got lost in them. "What are you saying, Michael?"

Maybe he should have been nervous. But how could he be nervous when Emily had always been the only woman in his heart? What's more, he knew he couldn't wait any longer. Even if she still seemed to want to try to avoid everything that had lain between them since they were kids, he had to get it out into the open. Just one glance down at the wedding told him that.

It wasn't just that her sisters all had their own lives now. It wasn't just that Emily had done everything she had said she was going to do to protect them and see them forth into the future. That made it sound as if her sisters had been a weight that had been holding Emily back, and that wasn't true. Michael cared about all of them too much to think that way.

Most of all, today's wedding proved just how well things could work out when people finally went after what they wanted. Brian was with Morgan because he hadn't given up. Hanna was with Joel because she'd told him how she felt about him. Rachel had gone after Nicholas on a *Jet Ski*. Even Paige—shy, reserved Paige—had been prepared to say on national television what she felt for Christian.

If they could each do that, then surely

Michael could say what he felt about Emily here and now. After all, it wasn't as if he'd ever doubted what he felt. He'd just been waiting for the perfect moment.

And this felt like the closest they were ever going to get to that perfect moment. There was no better reminder of the importance of love than having all her sisters happy around her, and she finally—*finally*—had no responsibilities left to compromise her own happiness.

It had to be today.

It had to be *now.*

"I love you."

The three little words were out in a second, and in that second, Michael knew he'd been carrying his love for Emily around as a secret for far too long.

Her eyes went wide, and even though her gasp was soft, he heard it.

"I love you," he said again. "I've loved you for years. And I think you care about me, too."

"Of course I care about you," she said. "But—" She faltered, as if she couldn't find the right words. "But you lived with us so long that you're practically family."

"I'm *not* family," Michael insisted. "I'm a man who loves you. A man who is standing here telling you that he wants to spend the rest of his life with you." He gently cupped her cheek, stroking her soft skin with the pad of his thumb. "I *know* you feel the same way. We've both been dancing around this for so long."

"You know I don't dance," Emily said, obviously trying to diffuse the situation with humor, the way she'd done so many times in the past whenever they'd come dangerously close to this moment.

She'd make a joke, or find something that urgently needed doing, or bring one of her sisters into the conversation. Anything to keep from acknowledging the truth. It was part of the reason he'd brought her up here in the first place. He'd not only wanted to take her away from those distractions, but he'd also wanted to show her that there wasn't any reason to keep resorting to them.

He moved closer, drawing her against him. "I love you," he said again, intending to keep saying it over and over until she finally believed him. "I love everything about you, even your two left feet."

She was silent for a few seconds, and Michael held his breath. He knew he had to give her enough time to think through what she really felt, but he couldn't help but pray she'd stop fighting her feelings for him, right here, right now.

"Michael." He'd watched her work with enough students over the years to know when she was using her counselor voice. She was obviously trying to let him down gently as she said, "I know how easy it is to get swept up in a day like today. You've seen everyone else pairing up, so you think that since we're the last two left we're going to hook up. But it doesn't work like that. We aren't going to get a happy-ever-after by default."

"No," he agreed, "happy-ever-after happens when two people who care about one another finally admit it rather than continuing to steer clear of their attraction and love for each other the way they have for years."

Was it so hard for her to believe that he could feel this way? Had she really not noticed all those times he'd found excuses to come around the Walker house? Yes, he'd lived there as a teenager, and yes, he'd been like a brother to her sisters, but it had never been like that for him with Emily.

"You've helped all your sisters to be that happy. Why not grab that happiness for yourself?"

He swore he saw something flash in her eyes—something that looked like the love he was hoping she'd return. Too quickly, however, she forced it away. Tried to force *him* away, too, as she slid out of his arms.

"It's been a long day. An emotional day. But when you wake up tomorrow, you're going to realize that you don't love me, not really. You're going to see that this was a mistake. And then we'll both be glad that neither of us took this any further so that our friendship doesn't have to suffer."

Michael worked hard to push back his frustration as he said, "I'll always be your friend, Emily. But no matter what I have to do, or how long it takes, I promise that I'm going to *prove* to you that I love you. And I'm also going to prove that you feel the same way about me."

CHAPTER THREE

Emily let Michael lead her back down toward the noise and the excitement of the wedding, her heart pounding extra hard, even though they were headed downhill now.

It felt as if an electric charge was sparking between them as they walked back in the twilight. Michael had his hand on her arm, and she was hyperaware of everything about him. For just a moment, it was almost possible to let herself see that he wasn't the teenage boy they'd taken in anymore, but a wonderful, handsome, amazing man walking beside her. If she'd met him in a bar...

Emily almost laughed out loud at that thought. When did she ever go to bars?

It was just that everything suddenly felt so topsy-turvy inside of her. Ever since that moment on the hill when Michael had said, *I love you.* Actually, before that—when he'd looked at her as if she was everything to him right after Morgan and Brian had said their vows.

But despite the fact that he'd repeated those same three little words of love again and again and again until her head—and heart—were spinning with them, she'd promised herself for ages that she would *never* go there. Allowing herself to fall for Michael would make things too complicated. Horribly complicated.

Because what if she and Michael weren't able to make things work? It would ruin everything. Not just their friendship—the most important one she had—but also every family gathering, even just those days when he was working around the house fixing a leaky sink or when they were both volunteering for the same project in town.

Okay, so the truth was that when he'd been declaring himself to her, she'd felt elated for a few heady moments. Nearly bursting with a happiness that she almost couldn't control.

But then, close on the heels of that elation, anxiety had hit. She'd felt exposed. Nervous. And scared that Michael had come close—way too close—to tearing down the walls she'd built up around herself so she could stay strong for everyone after their mother passed away.

Somehow, Emily knew she'd have to make Michael understand that they couldn't risk everything. Especially not their friendship. But right in this moment, with everything inside of her still whirling like a tornado, she couldn't find the words.

"Congratulations, Tres," Michael said as they made their way through the crowd of dancers toward her father. "Morgan and Brian are a great couple."

William Walker III looked the way he always did—slightly balding, his glasses perched on the end of his nose. Emily could easily imagine her mother straightening his bow tie, and it not quite lasting for more than a few minutes. Today, though her father looked happy, there was a note of sadness there, too. The same sadness she'd been feeling about her mother's absence.

"Thank you," her father said to Michael as his gaze moved to the happy couple. "They truly are meant to be."

He turned back to look between her and Michael, and for a moment, she thought her father might be about to say that Emily and Michael were also meant to be. But when the band started up with a new song, her father said instead, "It's been a long time since I've danced at a wedding."

The note of sadness in his voice tore straight through Emily. So even though she was the Walker sister who *didn't* dance, she found herself saying, "Would you like to dance with me, Dad?"

His look of surprise was followed by a great big smile. "I would *love* to dance with you, honey."

She let her father lead her away from Michael—and, thankfully, her careening thoughts and emotions about him, as well—and into the middle of a big group of dancing wedding guests.

Her father moved her easily into the first few steps as the band played in the background. Around them, Morgan was at the heart of it all in Brian's arms, her long white dress swishing around her ankles. Hanna was sneakily trying to film the whole thing on her phone over Joel's shoulder. Rachel and Nicholas were twirling a laughing Charlotte between them. And Paige and Christian were inadvertently stealing the limelight by being the best two dancers out there as they did what looked like an Argentine tango.

As Emily danced with her dad, she couldn't help but wonder what it might be like to dance with someone else. Someone younger, someone muscular, but gentle. Someone who would look at her with piercing brown eyes.

Someone, Emily realized, who was a spot-on description of Michael Bennet. But she'd made up her mind to stay away from foolish thoughts like that, so she put even more effort toward forcing it out of her head than she had earlier.

"You dance beautifully, Emily," her father said. "Just like your mother."

"I think you have me confused with Paige," Emily said with a laugh. "I'm the only one who didn't get the Walker dancing DNA, remember?"

"Nonsense, you've always been a great dancer. Somehow you just always ended up on the sidelines bandaging all your sisters' bruises from their overenthusiastic ballet jumps."

Emily found herself relaxing a little as she finally settled in to enjoy this moment with her father. What had happened up there on the hill with Michael had been some sort of strange wedding-day aberration. This, however, was safe...apart from the possibility of treading on her father's feet.

Emily remembered her father dancing with her mother. They'd always looked so happy together, whether swaying in each other's arms or just being together at home.

"Are you enjoying the wedding, honey?"

Emily immediately thought of Michael, which sent her back into an internal tizzy, but she made herself smile at her father. "It's turned out so beautifully, and Morgan and Brian seem really happy with everything."

"The vows were lovely."

When had they been reduced to this? To small talk about small stuff? Why did it so often feel like there were things they couldn't say to each other? Why wasn't she telling him about Michael? Asking him for advice? Or even just some reassurance that the complicated mess of feelings currently bubbling up inside her were actually not real and—

"Weddings always remind me so much of your mother," her father said with a sigh.

All along, she'd known this was the answer to her questions, hadn't she? He should have been more of a father to her and her sisters after their mother died. Only, he'd been so destroyed by his wife's death that he hadn't been able to be there for his daughters. They'd all been destroyed, but all of them had eventually learned to live again. All of them, except for her father.

"We can stop dancing if you like," Emily offered.

Tres shook his head. "No. It's better than standing around by myself thinking of how proud Ellen would have been to see her girls so happy and in love—and how I wish she could be here to see all of you for herself."

Michael had said almost exactly the same thing to her, although he had said how proud *Emily* should be, rather than her mother.

"Do you really think Mom would have been proud of us?"

"Absolutely," her father said as the band changed to another song and they moved straight into the next dance. "She would have been proud of all of you. Especially you, and the job you did looking after your sisters while I..."

While he'd fallen apart.

Emily could remember every single horrible moment of the day they'd been told that their mother had died. The crying faces of her little sisters, the way Grams' beautiful face had crumpled so that she'd suddenly looked a decade older.

But mostly Emily could remember her father becoming a walking shell of himself. His grief had made him forget that he was a father and left him remembering only how much he was hurting.

"Is everything on track for the school trip to Italy?" Emily asked, hoping to distract him.

Her father's bleak expression brightened a little. "It better be since we're leaving tomorrow. I just need to make sure that we come back with the same number of students that we leave with. Which can be harder than you'd think when it comes to places like Venice. Are you sure you won't come this time?" He often asked Emily that question when he was about to set off on one of his adventures.

Emily smiled, but shook her head. "I just don't think I can get away—especially with such late notice."

"Are you sure?" He didn't usually push her, but today he said, "You don't need to worry about your sisters. Grams is going off to do interviews on the mainland with Hanna and Joel, and the school is on spring break. I know it's late notice, but you should really think about it. I could call the tour organizer right now. I'm certain he could open up a spot for you."

"Thanks, Dad, but I'm looking after the farm while Morgan's away on her honeymoon. Now that spring is here, a lot of visitors are coming over to the island, so I volunteered to lead a few homestead tours."

"You couldn't get someone else to do those tours?"

"Everyone else has plans." She forced another smile. "I'm happy to do it." Just as she'd always been happy to take care of her sisters while her father had been breaking down.

Stop it, she firmly told herself as she

deliberately loosened her grip on her father's shoulders. This was not the time to be thinking about the past. She was at her sister's wedding and should be filled with nothing but joy.

But, sometimes, these feelings and memories had a way of popping up when she least expected them. Her dad had barely been able to face life on the island after her mother's death and had constantly been running off on trips abroad, leaving her and her sisters under the care of Grams. Even now, years later, he came around to Grams' house only on special occasions, preferring, instead, to live in his own small apartment. He hadn't abandoned them, exactly. When they'd been younger, he'd made sure they had everything they needed, and he'd taken care of all the bills. He was always so kind and gentle when he was with them, but the truth was that he had really missed out on watching them grow up.

For Emily, it had often felt as if she'd lost both parents.

"I know how hard it was for you looking after your sisters," he said, obviously guessing what she was thinking. He stopped dancing and told her, "It is something I will regret for the rest of my life. I'm so sorry I put you in that position."

Already topsy-turvy from Michael's pronouncement of love on the hill, Emily was now even more stunned by her father's apology. So stunned that it took several long moments for her to find her voice. "I understand why you had to stay away so much, Dad. At least, I think I do. It was hard on all of us. But, really, I didn't mind looking after the girls...most of the time anyway. I've always been good at looking after them."

He smiled. "Yes, you have." They began dancing again. "You know, honey, the older you get, the more you remind me of your mother."

"We all look like Mom," Emily pointed out, because, after all, she and her sisters shared many of the same features.

"I don't just mean physically. You have that same sense of calm grace. That same sense of control. Ellen was always the one who told me that things would work out, even right up to the end when she was so sick."

Her father had said some difficult things to her today, and now Emily knew it was her turn to ask him some difficult questions. Ones she'd always wanted to ask. "What's it like for you now? Does it still hurt just as badly, even after all this time?"

He was silent for a long moment, before finally saying, "I think some things will always hurt." But then he put on a smile, the same one she had been trying to wear herself, as he said, "But today isn't a day for talking about pain and sadness, is it?" Her father shot a look at Michael, who was standing over by the side of the dance floor watching them. "I'm wondering why he brought you over to me instead of dancing with you himself."

For a moment, Emily thought about telling her father everything Michael had said. *I love you.*

I've loved you for years. And I think you care about me, too. But she had always been the one other people went to, rather than the other way around.

Thankfully, before she had to try to answer her father's question about why she wasn't in Michael's arms right now, the caterer rushed over to ask her a question, so her father escorted her off the dance floor. But even as she was telling the woman where to locate the extra box of tea lights, Emily was wondering—what would it be like to love someone that much? To love another person to the point where they became your entire world?

As far as Emily was concerned, the thought of loving someone to the point where losing them left a gaping hole that rendered you incapable of living your life and getting back to normal was a frightening thought. So frightening that she got shivers just thinking about ever risking herself like that—risking losing who she was and then being unable to deal with all the things everyone depended on her for.

Almost automatically, she glanced across at Michael.

No. *No way.* She could never allow herself to risk ending up like her father.

So deeply, so wholly in love, that she would never recover if she lost it.

CHAPTER FOUR

Michael had loosened his tie and nursed his drink as he'd watched Emily dance with her dad. At first, she'd seemed happy. But then her expression had shifted to confusion...and then to sadness. Almost as if her happiness was draining away a little at a time.

He'd managed to see her face only in glimpses during the dance, but it had been obvious that Emily and her father were engaged in a serious conversation, one that had made her expression transform step by step, turn by turn. He knew she'd felt a bit off-kilter after they'd come down the hill—after he'd said *I love you* over and over in the hopes of getting her to believe that he meant it. But he definitely wouldn't have let her father steal her away for a dance if he'd thought Tres would upset her further.

Michael had wanted to break into their dance

and steal her back from her father. But he knew she'd *never* forgive him if he made a scene at her sister's wedding. The moment they stopped dancing, however, he headed straight toward her.

Before he could take more than a few steps, however, Emily's grandmother intercepted him.

Seeing that Emily was discussing something with the caterer, he smiled down at Ava Walker, thinking, as he always did, that she still had *it*. Even in her early eighties, she could dance rings around just about anyone.

Without a word, she held out her hands and took him with her onto the dance floor. Despite his concern about Emily, he was glad to be spending time with one of his favorite people in the world.

"You are a popular dance partner today, aren't you, Grams?"

"It seems so." Ava smiled as she said it.

"And I'll bet everyone here has been wanting to talk to you about your documentary, haven't they?" Emily's youngest sister, Hanna, had filmed a brilliant documentary about the six-decades-long Walker-Peterson feud, of which Ava Walker had ended up at the center of simply by falling in love with William. The press had been eating up the story for months, especially once they met Ava and saw how sparkling and beautiful she was.

But when Ava raised an eyebrow at him instead of replying to his question about the film, he knew he wasn't going to get away with diverting her from the questions he could see in her eyes. Michael might not actually be part of the Walker family, but Ava had always treated him as if he were her grandson, and he loved her dearly for that.

"I think we should have a little heart-to-heart, honey." She paused as if to let him take a moment to prepare himself for what she was about to say. "I saw you and Emily earlier, standing together at the top of the hill. You finally told her how you feel, didn't you?"

Michael almost tripped over his feet. Over the years, he had been amazed by how often Grams had known exactly what her grandchildren were thinking, sometimes even before they did themselves.

"How did you know?" he asked her, though he'd long suspected Ava could see straight through to what was in his heart for her oldest granddaughter.

Ava smiled, moving through another few steps with him. "Honestly? How could I *not* know? I've seen both of you casually date other people, but they never seemed to 'take'. You always came back to one another, even though I could tell you never talked about your feelings for one another and it was always just as friends. Plus, from the way you were holding her hands on that hill and how close you were standing to one another... Well, I can't imagine you were talking about the view."

It was Michael's turn to smile. "You don't

miss a thing, do you?"

"There's no secret to it," Grams said. "You just have to pay attention to someone for a long time. You have to care about them enough to want to do that. The way I know you pay close attention to Emily and know every little thing about her."

What Ava was saying was true. Seeing Emily almost every day, living close to her, spending so much time with her, loving her for all these years, he knew the precise lines that formed in her features when she frowned at something one of her sisters had done. The small half turn of her head that said she was really listening, even when she pretended not to. And the fact that she would never accept help when it was offered, treating any kind of assistance almost as an affront to her ability to cope.

"I would have to be a blind old woman not to see how much you love my granddaughter, Michael." Ava smiled at him, a warm smile that told him how much she cared for him. "Her sisters all see it, too."

Michael raised an eyebrow at that. Grams knowing everything about everyone in her house made perfect sense. But Morgan, Hanna, Paige, and Rachel being in on it, too?

"They haven't said anything to me."

"Perhaps they've been a little preoccupied with their own lives. Especially lately."

Grams looked over to where Brian and Morgan were standing beside each other, holding hands and kissing as they got ready to cut the cake. Charlotte was following just a pace or two behind to make sure that she was the first in line while Nicholas and Rachel looked on indulgently. Joel was helping Hanna film the moment, while Christian and Paige seemed to be dodging the cameras off to the side as they also stood with their arms around each other.

"Or maybe," Grams continued, "they didn't think it was their place to say anything."

He couldn't quite believe that one. "I can't think of the last time the four of them have held back on their opinions of me."

"Morgan really didn't like that tie you wore the other night, did she?" Ava said with a sparkling laugh that turned heads.

He laughed, too, before saying, "She cut it off of me with scissors."

A few moments later, however, Grams was looking serious again. "I suspect the real reason none of them have said anything to you or Emily is because they all hope that eventually the two of you will work things out. We all do. But the truth is that some things just have to take their course, no matter how long it takes." She put her hand over his and squeezed. "I know how long you've waited and how hard it's been for you." The look she gave him was one of pure love. "But some things are just inevitable."

Inevitable? Michael desperately wanted to believe that was true.

No, he thought with a shake of his head. He *knew* the love he felt for Emily was true. What he needed was for Emily to see it, too. Not only how much he loved her, but also how much she loved him.

"Besides, I know what a romantic you are, Michael. Now that all of Emily's sisters have found their own happily-ever-afters, how can you not want yours to finally come true?"

Michael's construction business was anything but romantic. He spent all his time doing practical things with wood and brick, glass and steel. Everything was straightforward, and there were no real mysteries, which was why he said, "I never thought I'd ever hear anyone accuse me of being a *romantic*."

"Of course you're a romantic. And it's not a bad thing, honey. Quite the opposite—I think it's absolutely wonderful. It's no wonder Morgan's wedding brought out the grand gesture in you. It's the same way weddings always bring my son to tears and have me hunting out the best-looking young men in the crowd to dance with."

"Including me?"

"How do you know I'm not talking about dancing with Christian?" Grams teased. "Especially now that Paige has taught him how to be so light on his feet."

"So light that something tells me she won't let anyone, not even her own grandmother, cut in right now," Michael pointed out with a teasing grin of his own.

What must it be like to be that close to someone, he wondered. To love them so much that just the thought of being apart from them made you ache inside.

But the truth was that Michael already knew the answers to those questions. He'd always known, ever since the first day he'd set eyes on Emily Walker.

"All right," he conceded, "maybe I am a romantic."

"But you're also practical. You know Emily so well that you know that she would never put herself ahead of her sisters. This wedding was your first big chance to really let her know what you feel. Of course you had to take that chance and declare yourself. And I'm glad you did, because Emily *needed* to hear it. She might not have been *prepared* for it, but she needed to hear it. And you needed to say it."

Ava was right. The need to tell Emily how he felt had been bubbling up inside of him for what felt like forever. He had been holding it back for as long as he could, and today, seeing so many of the other Walker sisters happy, seeing the men who loved them happy, he simply hadn't been able to stop himself from saying anything any longer.

"She didn't believe me," Michael blurted out. "She told me that I was just getting caught up in the moment and that I couldn't possibly love her. But I know what I feel about her. How I've always felt about her. I love her. With everything I am." He looked over Ava's shoulder at where Emily was now discussing something with the lighting coordinator while looking at the screen of an iPad. "I told her that I would prove my love to her, and that I would make her believe it's true when I say *I love you.*"

"Oh, honey, I have no doubt at all that you will be able to prove that to her. All she has to do is open her eyes and really let herself see what the rest of us already do."

"I also told her," he admitted in a low voice, "that I would prove that she loves me, too."

He was surprised when Ava laughed out loud. "You really are the best man in the world for her. Never forget that, no matter how frightened she must have been at hearing your declaration." But Ava's smile fell away as she told him, "I'm afraid that after everything life has thrown at Emily, it's easier for her to believe that you *don't* love her. Otherwise, she has to start thinking about everything she feels...and everything she stands to lose." Grams shook her head and sighed. "Unfortunately, it's so much safer just to look after everyone else's lives rather than put her own heart on the line and risk getting hurt."

"I don't want to hurt her, Grams. That's the very last thing I want."

"I've seen you spend sixteen years tying yourself in knots, trying to avoid doing just that. I know you're not about to start now. But sometimes...sometimes the path to true happiness is a little painful. And sometimes we need to tear down parts of what's there that aren't working before we can build something new and beautiful."

That was an idea Michael was very familiar with—working construction on an island full of historic buildings meant occasionally having to pull things apart to create something better. He also knew that it hadn't been easy for Ava to be caught up in the island feud when she fell in love with William. But Michael was certain that Ava wouldn't have changed a thing, or missed out on loving him, for anything.

"I've always known you two would be friends forever," Ava said in a gentle voice as their dance came to an end, "but now that you've finally taken this step today of confessing your feelings to my granddaughter? Well, I'm going to finally confess mine to you. I'm hoping for something more than *just friends* for you and Emily. Much more."

He smiled down at the woman who had taken him in at a time in his life when it had felt like he'd lost absolutely everything. "I'm hoping for the very same thing, Grams. For so much more that Emily will never again be able to doubt my love for her...or hers for me."

CHAPTER FIVE

Michael loved Ava Walker dearly. She'd always been there for him, and now that he was a grown man, things were no different.

As soon as their dance ended, Charlotte grabbed her hand, and now Ava was having the time of her life teaching her granddaughter the intricate steps of the samba. Things would be different in the big Walker house now that all the sisters had moved out, and he wondered what the future held for Ava...just as he wondered what the future held for him and for Emily.

Once upon a time, when he was a child, he'd assumed life moved in a linear fashion. You played with your friends, went to school, got a job, fell in love, and had a family. But sixteen years ago, he'd learned that life wasn't at all linear. Not when one horrible moment could make your entire life crumble around you.

Ava and the rest of the Walkers had helped

him through his pain.

But no one had helped him more than Emily.

* * *

Sixteen years ago...

"I'm so sorry for your loss, Michael," the woman said.

She explained who she was, something that sounded official, but right then Michael couldn't focus on much of anything. His parents had died the day before in a car crash, and now his house was full of people he barely knew, and all of them were eager to tell him just how sorry they were.

But being sorry didn't change anything, did it? Being sorry didn't make the car accident not happen. Being sorry didn't make his mom and dad reappear to fill the house with talking, and laughing, or even arguing. And being sorry sure didn't take away even a fragment of the pain that had settled inside him, tangling up his heart, refusing to budge.

There were so many people in the room. Distant relatives whom he hadn't seen in years and whose faces he barely remembered. Neighbors who had known his mom and dad, but whom he didn't know well, if at all. There were also a couple of "official-looking" people, such as the woman currently talking to him.

He didn't want any of them here. He didn't want them in his parents' house, saying empty, meaningless things about loss and healing while his mom and dad were gone forever.

"Yeah, sure," Michael said when the woman finally stopped talking. "I'm going to get a drink of water."

As he headed to the kitchen with his head down, even though it felt like there was a hard-rock band playing inside his skull, he still couldn't help but overhear what people were saying about him and his parents.

"How could they have been driving like that?"

"The house will have to be sold, of course. A teenager can't look after it all on his own."

"Where is he going to go now?"

Eventually, the fragments of conversation blended into a dark certainty that was bigger than the sum of its parts. A certainty that everything that had happened the day before was not the end of Michael's problems, but just the beginning.

And that even when it felt like the world should have already completely fallen apart, the worst was yet to come.

He slipped out the back door before anyone noticed, setting off down the street, not really knowing where he was going. Just as long as it was away from the house that should have felt so safe, but now felt more like a hole into which he was about to fall, being pushed slowly toward it by well-meaning people telling him how sorry they were for his loss.

Moments later, Michael's heart stalled in his chest. Emily Walker was making her way along the road from the opposite direction, golden-haired and beautiful. She was walking toward him the way she had ever since they were little children meeting for a playdate at the midpoint between their two houses, holding their moms' hands. Moms who were both gone now.

He could see that midpoint on the sidewalk now, a patch of sidewalk in front of a vacant lot and next to the right turn that led toward the center of town. A small signpost, pointing to a couple of the island's attractions, also marked the spot.

For years, they'd made a game out of trying to meet exactly at the midpoint, sometimes making it easy for one another, more often racing to it. Recently, she'd grown tall and graceful, easily able to stride across the distance, so he walked a bit quicker.

Today, Emily met him precisely in the middle, throwing her arms wide and hugging him.

Michael waited for her to say all the same stupid things as everyone else. But Emily still didn't say anything. She just held on to him, pressing him tight against her.

She was the only one who knew just what he needed right then. They'd told one another everything growing up. And, of course, Emily had experienced her own tragedies. Michael had been there when she'd found out that her mother had died. With her sisters around her, she hadn't let herself break down in front of them, even as her sisters all fell apart. Instead, she'd made sure to keep them together as a family, even through the horrible crisis. Michael had been the one to hold her when she'd been ready to cry in secret over the loss of her mom.

Now, it seemed, it was her turn to hold him.

"Come on," Emily said. "We'll go to my house."

Michael couldn't get words past the lump in his throat, so he just walked beside her while she held his hand. The best part about being with Emily was that, at a time like this, he knew he didn't have to say anything. And she didn't have to ask how he was feeling, because she knew.

Finally, though, when he had managed to swallow the lump down, he had to say, "What was it like? After..."

"It was horrible," she told him in a soft voice. "And it stayed like that for a long time."

She was the first person who had been honest with him today, and even though it was painful to hear, he'd never appreciated her honesty more. Almost as much as he appreciated the fact that she was there for him, just as she'd always been.

He heard her swallow hard before she told him, "I'm sure Grams has got lunch going."

Even if Grams wasn't there, Michael knew Emily would make food for him and everyone else.

They walked up to the Walker house, going through to the kitchen. Emily's sisters were at home, along with Ava, who was showing Paige a dance move in the living room. Her father, Michael's English teacher from school, was there, too, reading with Hanna, the youngest of the sisters.

They all looked up at once when he and Emily entered the kitchen. He was certain that one of two things would happen: Either they would all start talking like everyone back at his house, or they would make him go back home to the wake.

But before anyone could say a word, Emily took charge. "Is there any of that soup left, Grams?"

"Of course there is. Come and sit down, Michael."

He sat, but Emily didn't leave his side. Rachel moved over to touch his shoulder lightly, before heading out of the kitchen.

"Do you want to play, Michael?" Hanna asked. At just seven, she was the youngest of the sisters.

"Not today, darling," her father said, before Michael could reply. "Paige, why don't you take Hanna and Morgan over to the dance studio?"

Paige nodded, her big eyes sad as she looked at Michael, and her sisters followed her out willingly.

"I'm going to have to call your house," Mr. Walker said. "Just to let them know where you are."

"But, Dad," Emily said quickly, "if you do that, they'll just come get him."

Her father looked at her and then at Michael. "I can understand not wanting to be there right now. But I've still got to let them know he's here."

"Dad—"

"Emily," Ava Walker said. "You know your father has to call. He's got to do the right thing. Don't you, William?"

William. Michael didn't think he'd ever heard anyone call Mr. Walker by his first name. He was always Mr. Walker, or Tres, or "Emily's dad".

"Because he's done such a great job of doing the right thing so far," Emily snapped back.

It was weird for Michael, hearing her talk to her own father like that, the disappointment in her tone unmistakable.

Ava looked at her sharply. "Emily, that was uncalled for."

"Really? I'd say that it was *completely* called for."

Michael pushed back from the table. "Emily, your grandmother's right. I mean...at least you have a dad. I'm sorry, if I'm causing trouble being here—"

"You're not causing any trouble at all, Michael," Mr. Walker said, waving him back into his seat.

Emily reached for his hand and wouldn't let go. "I want Michael to stay, Dad. He *needs* to stay. Here. With us. No matter what anyone else wants him to do, he belongs here with us now."

All Michael wanted was to stay with them. Not just for the next few minutes, but permanently. Apart from his own home, which was now overrun with long-lost relatives and strangers, the Walker house was the only home he'd ever known.

Thankfully, Tres didn't so much as pause before nodding and saying, "Mom, can you handle things here for a moment while I make the call?"

"Of course," Ava replied. "Michael, sit back down and have something to eat while Tres lets them know just how much we'd like you to stay with us."

A few moments later, they all heard Emily's father speaking on the phone. "This is Tres Walker from up the street. I wanted you to know that Michael is over at our place. Yes, my daughter brought him home. They're friends from school." He listened for a moment or two. "Yes, I understand, but for the moment...no. No," he said again in an even stronger voice. "I really don't think that's a good idea. Yes, I'm perfectly aware of what I'm saying, and I know exactly how this situation works."

There was a note of authority in his voice that Michael hadn't heard from Mr. Walker outside of school. On the occasions when Michael had seen him around the Walker house, he'd seemed nice but always a little bit sad. Michael had never seen or heard him this much in control.

As they listened to the call, Emily was right there beside him, still holding his hand, quiet yet fiercely protective. When Hanna ran back in with one arm in her coat, wanting to hug Michael, it was Emily who gently pulled her sister from him, helped her with her coat, and sent her back in the direction of the others.

"Yes," Emily's father said from the other room. "I understand that you need to get back to the mainland and that you want to take him with you. However, have you or anyone else actually asked Michael's opinion on the matter?" He paused for a moment before saying, "I can see why you might have thought that there isn't another choice. However, I would like to provide one. My house. My family. We want him here." Michael's heart was flipping around like crazy in his chest as Tres said, "I really do feel that it's the best option. He should stay on the island to finish school. He should stay with us."

Emily tugged silently on Michael's hand, pulling him away from the table. She led him through the twists and turns of the big old house and up to her bedroom, one that was clean and neatly kept, with well-read books stacked carefully on shelves.

"It sounds like Dad is actually going to come through on this."

The note of bitterness that had crept in whenever she spoke about her father since her mother had died was barely noticeable for once. It seemed that this time Emily approved of what her father was doing.

"Thanks for getting him to agree to take me in." Tres Walker was a good man, but he would never have done what he'd just done if Emily hadn't pushed him toward doing it.

"If this plan works," she said, "you'll be

spending a lot more time around here. Will you be okay with that?"

Michael would be so much more than okay with it. He would much rather live with people he knew than with relatives he really didn't know at all. Especially if it meant he got to stay with Emily.

Because even then, he loved her with everything he was.

CHAPTER SIX

Present day, Morgan and Brian's wedding...

The wedding planner stepped up to the band's PA system. "Ladies and gentlemen, the bride and groom would like to get some photos of you dancing. Could we please all move to the dance floor with our partners?"

Emily's sisters were already dancing with the men they loved. They didn't need an announcement to do what came naturally. Even little Charlotte had found a couple of teenagers to dance with, and she was showing them the moves she'd learned at Grams and Paige's dance studio. The teens applauded, then showed her a few moves of their own.

"Shall we, Emily?" Michael drew her into his arms without waiting for an answer.

They'd come to the wedding as friends, and as the maid of honor and best man, and now...well, now Emily wasn't sure if she could stand there comfortably in his arms while the photographers snapped pictures. Not with so much emotion spinning and tangling around inside her.

But before she could try to protest, they were out on the crowded dance floor and the photographers were snapping the pictures the bride and groom wanted.

For her sisters, the moment looked so utterly romantic. Morgan and Brian were so utterly in love that they likely wouldn't have noticed if an entire marching band were passing next to them just then. Paige and Christian were dancing so close, and in such perfect synchronization, that it was hard to see where one ended and the other began. Hanna and Joel were holding one another tightly and laughing as the photographers got their shots. Rachel and Nicholas were dancing with their usual enthusiasm and athleticism, heedless of the danger of crashing into other couples.

Only Emily was tense. As if she were poised to run and was only just barely able to keep from pushing out of Michael's arms and running as fast, and as far away, as she could.

It wasn't because she didn't love him. On the contrary, she was very much afraid that she did.

Too much.

And too deeply.

Which made it *far* too much of a risk. For both of them.

"How long do you think they're going to keep us out here like this?" Emily asked.

"They're wedding photographers," he replied. "I'm pretty sure they think they're in charge of the whole day." But from the serious way he was staring into her eyes, she didn't think he was thinking about the photographers. No, she was almost positive he was thinking about *them.*

Normally, they were able to give each other easy smiles. Because they were friends. But today...today it didn't feel like anything would ever be easy between them again. All because he'd ruined the chances of easy smiles, and friendly dances, when he'd said *I love you.*

As the photographer came toward them and the crowd of dancers seemed to close in tighter, Emily ended up pressed tightly enough to Michael to feel every nuance of his muscles beneath his suit. She knew he was in great shape from his construction work and the run he went for every afternoon—and she might have even secretly daydreamed about a moment like this in the past. But right now the last thing she could do was give in to her secret longings for him.

She tried to put some space between them, but the photographer immediately scolded her. "You look like you don't even want to dance with him when you pull back like that. It will be a *terrible* picture for your sister and her husband, and I know you can't possibly want that, can you?"

Oh, brother. Yes, the photographers definitely

thought they were in charge. But because she didn't want to ruin her sister's wedding, she had no choice but to move close to Michael again. Back into his strong arms, so close that she could feel his heart beating against hers and breathe in his clean, masculine scent.

"Do they need to take quite so *many* photographs of us?" Emily muttered.

"You're Morgan's eldest sister and maid of honor. Of course they're going to want plenty of pictures of you. Besides," he said in a low tone that simmered all along her spine, "you're the most beautiful woman here."

Yet again, he stunned her. Both with his words *and* the sheer longing in them. A longing he was no longer trying to hide.

"Morgan is the most beautiful woman here," she replied, wishing her voice didn't sound quite so breathless. It wasn't okay to be breathless around Michael. For so long she'd succeeded at pushing away her desire for him. Today of all days, she couldn't finally break. "She's the bride. It's the rule."

"Rules are made to be broken."

A few moments later, when the announcer cut in to say that they'd reached the end of the dance photography, Emily knew it had been a really close shave. Because she couldn't have spent another moment in Michael's arms, not when all of her secret longings were bubbling up from moment to moment. Unfortunately, as if Murphy's Law were the rule of the day, the wedding planner had another message.

"If we could have everyone in the bride's family, and their partners, over by the arbor, we just have a handful more shots to take."

Steeling herself not to do anything to ruin her sister's big day, she let Michael hold her hand as they walked over to the arrangement of chairs by the roses. Morgan and Brian were seated in the middle, and everyone else was on either side of them. Her sisters were next to the men they loved, and Emily was next to Michael.

Emily had helped plan these pictures with Morgan. She had agreed that it made sense for her and Michael to sit together. But that was *before.*

Everything felt different now. After *I love you*.

Morgan and Brian were so perfectly happy today, and of course, Emily wished them every happiness in the future. But at the same time, she knew as well as anyone how quickly that happiness could be snatched away. How easily love could leave the kind of gaping hole it had left in her father after her mother's death...and how horribly unhappy it had made him.

She felt Michael's hand slide over hers. "Emily?" His voice was low enough that only she could hear it. "You look upset. You've looked upset ever since you danced with your father."

She knew she should be keeping a perfect smile on her face for the pictures. But how could she when Michael was right next to her and she couldn't find a way to close the lid he'd decided it was time to finally pry off?

"How could you?" she said in just as low a voice, while the photographers bustled about adjusting lights and her siblings talked with the men they adored. "How could you have said those things to me on the hill?"

He held her gaze, his as steady as hers was distraught. "Is it really such a surprise?"

"Okay," the photographer said, "can we have everyone looking this way?"

Emily turned and sat, facing forward, doing her best to whisper to Michael out of the side of her mouth.

"Today of all days, with Dad upset the way he always is at these things..."

"You know how much I respect him," Michael whispered back. "How much I owe him. But this is about us. *Just* us."

"Come on, everybody," the photographer said, and again, Emily knew he was talking specifically to her. "Let's see some big smiles."

Right then, Emily was the only one in the wedding party whose smile was faltering around the edges. Never in her life had she had to work at something as simple as smiling and having her photo taken with her family.

"Just a few more to go," the photographer said encouragingly. "Hold that pose."

Those few pictures felt like they took eons, and when they were finally cut loose, Michael reached for her hand before she could dart away and pulled her behind a rose bush where they could talk in relative privacy.

"If I thought that you would be happy with someone else, I'd back off. Even if I thought you really didn't want me, I'd back off. But I know you, Emily. I see how you react every time we're close together. Just like today when we were dancing, how your heartbeat sped up and your breath came faster. Just like mine did from holding you." His dark eyes held hers, as if he were daring her to lie and tell him it wasn't true. "If I thought you would be happy with me as the guy who lives down the street and just drops by for Sunday dinner and to fix things, I'd do that for you. But I *don't* think you want that. I think you want more."

He paused again, just long enough for her heart to leap all the way into her throat as he said, "Tell me the truth. Am I wasting my time? Are you looking for someone else? For a different man to love you—and for you to love right back?"

Emily's lips opened.

But nothing came out.

To her sisters, Michael had always been a surrogate big brother. Someone who would look out for them. Someone they could go to when they needed help. Someone to do the job when their boyfriends needed reminding to be polite, or to listen to them when they thought Emily wasn't being fair.

But with her and Michael, things had always been different. He'd been a friend, not a brother. And then, sometimes...sometimes she'd found herself dreaming of more. Of more than a friend.

Of what his kisses might feel like. And of what it might be like not just to let herself fall for him, but to fall all the way, head over heels, heart and soul.

All her life she'd been the strong one. The sensible one. But just then, when she heard a photographer say through the rose bush, "Where's Emily? We need to get a few shots of Morgan with all her bridesmaids now," she nearly fell to her knees in gratitude that the photographers she'd just wished would go away weren't actually done yet.

"I have to go. They need me."

But instead of letting her go, he continued to hold her hand for a long moment in which she couldn't look away from his eyes. She couldn't hide from everything he was now showing her. Not only how much he loved her, but also his clear determination not to give up. Finally, he lifted her hand to his lips for a kiss.

One that was easily the sweetest anyone had ever given her.

CHAPTER SEVEN

The day after Morgan and Brian's wedding, the Walker house was a hive of activity. Between organizing the wedding gifts, Charlotte running all over the place, and the phone ringing, the place had been a zoo. Grams had taken it all in stride, as usual, but Emily had felt a little frazzled. More than a little frazzled, actually, although she knew it wasn't just because of all the noise and chaos in the house.

No, it was the noise and chaos inside her head—and her heart—in the wake of Michael's declaration that had her feeling so off-kilter.

Day two after the wedding, however, was different. The silence was so absolute, in fact, that it had woken Emily up even though she'd been planning to stay in bed on the first official day of spring break. Then again, since she'd never been able to sleep in before, she supposed today wasn't likely to be any different.

A few minutes later she was standing in the kitchen in her robe and old, but extremely comfortable, slippers, sipping coffee. And all she could think was that the quietness of the old house was almost deafening.

There was no one here, for once, which almost never happened. Or certainly not for more than an hour or two, anyway. Yes, there might be times when Grams and Paige were both at the dance studio, but nine times out of ten, one of her sisters or a friend would choose that moment to drop by. And that was if Emily was even at home. Sometimes, the line of students wanting to talk with her after hours seemed infinite.

Today, though, there was just silence. Morgan and Brian had left last night on their honeymoon to Rio de Janeiro. Their father was halfway to Italy for the school trip. Rachel, Nicholas, and Charlotte were off filming their adventure TV show in Las Vegas, Nevada. Grams, Hanna, and Joel had taken a ferry to Seattle for another round of press interviews about their documentary.

"Even Paige has gone," Emily said to the empty house. "How did *that* happen?"

But Emily knew perfectly well how it had happened. Paige had fallen deliriously in love with a Hollywood star who loved her back just as much. They had left the island last night to get back to Los Angeles to attend a glitzy Hollywood event that Emily had once assumed Paige would always hate. But things like that didn't bother her anymore, as long as Christian was by her side.

Emily didn't begrudge Paige a moment of that happiness. She was glad her sister had found someone she loved that much and who obviously cared just as much about her. It was just...

Well, she thought with a sigh, it was just that she was so used to Paige always being around that she'd half-expected it would always be that way. The two of them rattling around the old Walker house under Grams' watchful gaze. Paige coming in late from the dance studio, or trying to talk them into watching one of her favorite dance musicals.

Just like she did every morning, Emily started pulling out ingredients. Pancakes sounded good today. There was nothing like a nice, big pancake breakfast to—

Emily stopped herself short, her hand still gripping the bag of flour. She'd set out enough flour, milk, butter, and eggs to produce pancakes for at least four people. More, actually, because she was used to people dropping in for breakfast without warning, and Paige always needed plenty of fuel for her dancing. But all the ingredients served to do today was remind her of just how empty the house was.

The sound of the kitchen door opening was so loud that Emily practically jumped out of her skin. Who could it be? Who was actually *left* on the island?

But she knew, didn't she? Knew that it had to be the one person she'd been waiting for all along.

Michael.

He looked good, just like he always did, even when he was simply wearing a casual shirt and jeans with his work boots. She, on the other hand, knew without a doubt that her robe and old slippers weren't cutting it. Worse, though, was the fact that she couldn't help wishing she'd actually brushed her hair and put on something nicer before coming downstairs, if only so that Michael would still think she was pretty.

Gorgeous was what he'd said, and thrill bumps ran over her skin every time she thought about the intense way he'd looked at her while saying it. As if he wanted to run kisses over every inch of her skin...

"Hi."

He'd been with her in the kitchen a thousand times or more. And yet, for the first time, she felt a little shy. And she couldn't figure out how to calm her racing heart, either.

"Hi."

His smile was warm. And strangely *normal* given what had gone down between them at the wedding.

This was the first time she'd seen him since Saturday, and a part of her had expected him to immediately make good on his vow to prove his love—and hers. Especially given the determination she'd seen in his eyes right before he'd lifted her hand to his lips for a kiss behind the rose arbor.

But he didn't have any flowers, and he clearly

wasn't trying to sweep her off her feet. On the contrary, he was simply standing there, saying, "Do you want to go get breakfast?"

"Breakfast?" Her brain couldn't quite catch up, not when she was busy getting lost in his eyes. Eyes that she'd never let herself get lost in before.

But in the *after*...

He gestured to the big empty table. "I figured you wouldn't want to bother cooking without everyone else here."

Emily didn't understand. Not just her own wildly careening feelings, but also what Michael was doing now...being so reasonable? Being so *normal*? What kind of guy declared his love for a woman one day and then carried on like nothing had happened the next?

Okay, so he was asking her out for breakfast versus eating here the way they normally did, but they'd had breakfast together in the Walker house so often that Emily often teased him that his own kitchen appliances must still be wrapped in plastic.

Maybe he'd rethought his declaration? Maybe he'd come over this morning not to prove to her that he loved her and she loved him, but to show her that she was right about the two of them just being good friends. Friends who went out to breakfast. Friends who didn't make each other's heart race. Friends who weren't dying to kiss each oth—

She barely stopped herself in time, barely managed to remember that this was *Michael*.

They'd been friends forever. And she couldn't let anything change that. No matter how much a part of her might be dying to do just that.

"Emily?"

His voice snapped her out of her musings, and she made herself smile. Another one of those smiles that used to come so easily but were now among the hardest things for her to pull off.

"Breakfast sounds good. Just give me a minute to throw some clothes on," she said, pleased that her voice sounded mostly normal.

"You mean the rest of Walker Island isn't getting to see the fuzzy slippers?"

"Walker Island isn't ready for the fuzzy slippers."

Phew, there they were, back to their old banter, as if nothing had happened. Emily went upstairs, dressing in a blue cashmere hoodie that matched her eyes, new jeans that Morgan had said looked amazing on her, and her boots.

She breathed a sigh of relief—*that* had been a narrow escape.

And yet...

She couldn't help but feel a small twist of disappointment that settled inside her as she checked herself in the mirror. The feeling that after everything that had been said yesterday, Michael *shouldn't* have just shown up like nothing had happened.

But what did she want? What did she expect? For Michael to show up with a seven-piece band? To send a skywriting airplane out into the sky to make a heart of smoke with her name in the middle of it?

Stop. She needed to stop freaking out and just go to breakfast and pretend nothing had happened and forget all about hearing Michael say *I love you*. Just like he clearly had. Because whatever had him in its clutches on Saturday—whether it was wedding romance or too much champagne—the fever had clearly passed.

They headed out of the house, walking toward one of the cafés along the docks, and were barely on their way when Emily got her first compliment on the wedding.

"It was just lovely," one of her neighbors said. "A really beautiful occasion."

That was all it took for the floodgates to open, as it seemed that every local they passed wanted to talk about it.

"You must be so proud," a painter said to Emily as she and Michael made their way past his studio near the docks. "Your daught—I mean, your sister looked lovely in her wedding dress."

"Morgan always looks lovely," Emily replied, ignoring the *daughter* slip as best she could.

"It's always so hard when they grow up, isn't it?" said one of the painter's friends.

Did none of these people know that she was one of the Walker *sisters*? Surely she didn't look old enough to be their mother. Then again, she had helped raise her younger sisters, so maybe it was no surprise that people thought of her that way. And she did feel incredibly proud of Morgan, the same way she felt proud of all the others.

"Your family is on a roll," the woman continued. "Will there be any more Walker weddings this year?"

"You'll have to check with my sisters on that."

The painter nodded to Michael. "You'd better snap this one up quickly now that she's the only available Walker sister left."

Wow. What was it with everyone? First they thought she was her sisters' mother and now they wanted to marry her off.

Thankfully, Michael simply said, "Have a nice day," then hustled them toward the docks. By the time they got to the café, she was dying for the kind of fried, fatty breakfast she usually tried to avoid.

"Do you have any plans for the week?" Michael asked after they finished recounting the wedding with all of the locals in the café and their meals arrived.

"I told Morgan that I'd help with the tours at her garden while she's gone." The tourists loved seeing where and how all the ingredients for Morgan's makeup line got developed.

"I promised Morgan that I'd help out, too."

"You did?" Why hadn't Morgan mentioned this to her?

Her family had never tried to matchmake before, but Emily suddenly wondered—had Walker wedding fever changed everything?

"I promised Brian I would help keep the plants thriving while they're away on their honeymoon." Michael smiled as he explained, "He was worried Morgan would spend all her time in Rio worrying about her herbs otherwise."

Emily laughed at that. Partly because she was sure Brian was going to give Morgan plenty of other things to think about on their honeymoon, but mostly because she could easily imagine her sister demanding regular updates on the state of her herbs.

"It looks like we're going to be seeing a lot of one another over spring break, won't we?"

"Looks like it," Emily said.

She studied his face for a long moment, trying to see if there was a hidden message, or any kind of clue that he was planning something. Was this the moment in which he'd surprise her again with a big romantic gesture to "prove his love"?

But he was tucking into his pancakes as if he didn't have a care in the world. Certainly not looking love-struck or angst-filled about whether or not she was about to accept his confession of love.

Which was good. Great, actually. Because everything was back to normal. Just her and her friend having breakfast together, with no romantic entanglements on the horizon.

With another sigh, Emily tucked into her own pancakes, working all the while to stuff back down the longing that had so foolishly bubbled up at the wedding.

CHAPTER EIGHT

The next day there were more people than Emily expected for the tour of Morgan's extensive herb and flower gardens. Some of the visitors were there for the history, some for the opportunity to tour a space that managed to be beautifully wild in spite of its careful cultivation, and a few were there simply because it was where TV star Morgan Walker had just gotten married.

Emily did her best to cater to all of them. "When our great-grandfather started growing berries, this is where he first started. He lived here, too, right next to the site of those first fields. We'll go see the place in a few minutes."

"He didn't live up at the Walker house in town?" one of the tourists asked.

Emily shook her head. "That came a little later, once his business took off and the town started to grow and more berry pickers and ferry workers settled on the island."

"Will we get a chance to see that house?"

"I'm sorry, it's a private home now." But even as she said it, she couldn't help but think that it was going to be a different kind of home now with just her and Grams living there.

"If you'll follow me to the far end of the field," Emily said, "we can talk about some of the varieties of berries grown on the island and the role my grandfather played in hybridizing some of them."

She caught sight of Michael as she led the group to the far end of the north field. He was trimming back plants as he worked to keep the berry brambles in check. He waved when he saw Emily, and she waved back. She noticed a couple of the female members of the group waved to him, as well. Quite hopefully, it seemed, given that they'd probably also noticed how good he looked in his plaid shirt, jeans, and work boots.

"Who's that?" one of them asked.

"That's Michael." Emily smiled as she said his name. "He often helps our family out with things."

"So he's your handyman?"

"No. He's..."

What *was* Michael, exactly? A close friend to her family? Their surrogate brother? Grams' foster grandson? The Walkers' regular gatecrasher at mealtimes? The man who kept their house from falling down around them?

Or was he more than that?

So much more...

"We shouldn't distract him," Emily said, pressing on. "He's got a lot to get through here, and so do we."

That was when she spotted the dog. It wasn't a big dog, maybe the size of a small Spaniel, although its breed seemed a lot less clear. It was one of those dogs that seemed to have a bit of everything crammed into its small frame. It had shaggy hair that had probably been white once, but was currently various shades of beige and brown. The poor thing was scruffy and tangled from being outside.

The dog was standing in the middle of a row of roses, looking at Emily with obvious interest, as though wondering what she was going to do next. When she took a step toward it, it disappeared back into the bushes, only to reappear farther along, still looking at her.

The dog was clearly a stray. Just one look was enough to tell Emily that it had been out in the open awhile, without anyone to take care of it. Emily loved dogs, but she had never gotten to spend much time around them given Paige's allergies.

She wanted to go over to make sure it was all right, but she couldn't leave the visitors to Morgan's farm hanging. Fortunately, Emily could see Michael was now watching the dog, too, and had moved to work fairly close to it.

"So over here, we have..."

The script she'd come up with for the tour came out automatically, which was just as well as she was busy trying to keep an eye on the dog. Emily watched as it made its way around the garden, sniffing at the growing herbs and flowers, occasionally glancing back in her direction as if to say, *I'm not going anywhere. I'm going to wait for you.*

"And that concludes our tour for today," Emily said at last, sighing inwardly with relief as the tourists made their way back to their cars.

Morgan's idea of opening up the old family homestead as an attraction might have been a good one from the point of view of preserving their family's history on the island, but today it had meant not being able to do the one thing Emily had wanted to do for the better part of an hour.

"Hello, boy. You must be lost." Emily made her way toward the dog, holding out her hand. This time, it didn't dart away, but moved forward cautiously instead.

"I was wondering how long it would take you to come over here once the tour was finished," Michael said, stepping beside her. The dog looked at him, but kept closer to Emily.

"You could have gone over to him," she pointed out.

"No," he said with a shake of his head, "I could tell he liked you more than me. Are you thinking about adopting him?"

"Adopting him?" Emily honestly hadn't gone there. Even as a little girl she'd known they couldn't have a dog without making Paige's eyes and nose run. "No, I can't. Paige is allergic to dogs, remember?"

Michael reached out, putting a hand on her arm. "Paige doesn't live there anymore. And she can put up with a dog when she and Christian come back to the island to visit and drop by the house. Besides, everyone knows how much you've always wanted a dog."

"Everyone?"

"Well," he said, his dark eyes holding hers, "*I've* always known. Why don't you just take him in? He's obviously in need of a good home, and I couldn't think of a better one than with you. I'm sure Ava will be fine with it. After everything else that has been in that house, do you think one little dog is going to make a difference?"

He had a point there. Her grandmother had put up with children, parties, and all kinds of chaos over the years. One small dog probably wasn't going to make any difference to her.

Even so, Emily knew that things had to be done properly. "I can't just take the dog and make him mine, Michael. He might have an owner somewhere looking for him. There might be people trying to find him."

The dog whined, coming close enough now to brush up against her legs. Michael looked from him to Emily. "He doesn't look much like he has just run off from someone, does he? He has obviously been out here awhile."

Emily took another long look at the dog. He truly did look scrawny and ill-fed, as if he'd been living out in the open for a while. Fortunately, though, he was friendly enough to let Emily stroke his back.

"Come on, Emily," Michael coaxed her. "You know you want to take him home."

He was right, she did. Very much. But she couldn't let herself get attached to the hope that this dog might become hers until she made sure it was actually possible. "We need to take him to the vet to check out his health and to see if he has a chip. If he does, the vet will probably be able to locate his owner."

Each time she said the word *vet*, the dog growled softly.

"I don't think he likes that word very much," Michael said.

"Well, tough." She knelt by the dog and continued stroking his fur gently. "Sometimes we have to do things we're afraid of because they're good for us. But I won't let anything bad happen to you. I promise."

Between them, they managed to coax the dog into Emily's car. They drove to the island's veterinary office, where they were quickly shown to Cameron Bainton's office. They both knew him from school, but neither had seen much of him over the years.

He smiled as Emily and Michael came in. "Emily, Michael, it's good to see you again. I saw the pictures of you and your family at the wedding, Emily. Everyone looked so happy. Now," he said with a look at the dog, "who's this little guy?"

"That's what we were hoping you could tell us, Cameron," Emily said. "We found him in Morgan's garden."

Cameron examined the dog with the thorough attention Emily remembered of him. He'd always paid attention in class and gotten good grades.

"Is it busy for you here as the only vet on the island?" Michael asked as Cameron continued his examination.

"Some days are busier than others, but we do get a lot of emergencies."

"Weren't you tempted to leave the island after finishing school to work in a bigger city?" Michael asked.

"Why would anyone want to leave the island?"

Emily smiled. She felt exactly the same way.

Cameron went back to examining the dog, who was squirming and trying to get off the examination table. Emily decided it would be best if she helped out by holding him in place. Fortunately, when she began to scratch his ears, he looked up at her with pure joy and relaxed.

"You stayed on at the school, didn't you, Emily?" Cameron asked while he worked.

"Yes, as a guidance counselor. I really enjoy working with the kids."

"It's good to have a job where you're making a difference. Something you love doing." From the way he smiled at her as he said it, Emily got the feeling that if she and Cameron had been alone, he might have said more than that. Maybe even asked her out.

"So," Michael interrupted, his voice a little gruffer than usual, "what's the verdict? Is the little guy okay?"

"He's not doing badly, considering that he's obviously been living rough. There aren't any major problems that I can see, and a few minor tests will tell us if there's anything we need to worry about. He's just a bit dirty and underfed. He needs care and love, but then, we could all do with that."

When he smiled at Emily again, this time she was *positive* that he was interested in her as more than a new client who had brought in a stray dog.

Interestingly, she was also positive that Michael's ruff was up a bit. As if he was jealous.

Turning her focus back to the dog, she asked, "Is he chipped so that we can find out who he belongs to?"

"There's no chip. My guess is that he's a stray who came over on one of the boats from Seattle. We have a real problem with that here on the island. The animals stow away or people bring them over and lose them. I could check with the local animal shelter and some vets on the mainland, but in the meantime, our little friend here has to go somewhere. I could call the animal shelter if you can't take him in."

"No," Michael said. "He'd be happier with you, Emily. We can all see that. He already adores you."

"Can we really just take him?" Emily asked as the hope she'd been trying to hold at bay blossomed.

"We?" He was looking from her to Michael as if trying to work out what sort of relationship they had.

Emily focused on the dog, ruffling his ears. "He'll go to the house with me," she clarified. "Plus, Grams will be there later this week." She looked into the dog's scruffy face. "How about it? Would you like to come home with me?"

The dog barked, and Emily took that to be a *yes*. She wasn't about to let a dog like this end up in a rescue shelter when she was in a position to help him—even if he might have an owner who would soon take him away from her.

"I'll let you know if I find out anything about a possible former owner," Cameron said. "It's probably best if you leave me your number, Emily, so that I can call you if I find out anything."

Emily stroked the dog's head. "We'll soon have you home, little guy. I hope you're going to like living with me for a while."

Michael smiled. "Something tells me that if you give this dog half the attention you've given everyone else in your life, he's going to be a very happy dog indeed."

CHAPTER NINE

"Thanks, Cameron," Michael said as they prepared to leave the clinic. "It was good seeing you again."

"You, too," Cameron said, although his comment seemed more directed at Emily than Michael. He had no doubt the other man would have asked her out if he weren't there. The only thing in question was—would she have said yes?

Michael had to work to push his jealous thoughts aside as Emily led the dog out to her car, a look of obvious happiness on her face. She couldn't stop smiling at the dog. He knew exactly how much she'd always wanted one of her own, and it was good to see her finally get her wish.

"You're going to a good home," Michael said, bending to scratch the dog's ears. It woofed softly in response.

"Well, just until we can find his owners," Emily reminded him, but she didn't say it with much enthusiasm.

Even though Cameron had just told them that the odds of finding any owners weren't great, she was clearly working to keep her emotions in check, rather than letting herself truly believe that she now had a dog.

Michael had come over to the house yesterday morning to set into motion the next step in his plan to woo her, but then he'd seen her standing there in the kitchen looking so lost. So sad. There had been so many changes for her already, with all of her sisters moving out in the past year. And just as he'd told Grams at the wedding, he couldn't stand the thought of doing anything to hurt Emily. So he'd deliberately held back again when he'd asked her to breakfast, all the while planning to begin wooing her in earnest today, after they both finished with their chores at the garden. But then they'd found the dog.

Clearly, trying to prove to Emily that he loved her—and that she loved him—was going to take a lot of time and patience. But he figured he could at least help things along a little for the dog.

"Have you thought of a name?"

"I don't know if I should give him one," she replied. "I mean, if his owners show up, he'll just end up confused by having two names." She gave the dog a long look. "But if no one shows up, I don't think it's fair to call him Boy forever."

Michael swore the dog shook his head just then, as if he could understand every word she was saying. He wondered if Emily saw it, too, because she smiled and said, "I think he looks like a Gus." The dog sat up straighter, as if he was already responding to his new name. And liked it. "There are so many things we need to do. We need to get a bowl, and a leash, and some dog food. We'll need to get some of the tangles out of your fur and give you a bath—"

Gus barked again. Did he understand the word bath the way he seemed to understand so many other things?

Michael reached out to put a hand on Emily's shoulder. "You'll be fine. You managed to bring up a whole house full of sisters. I'm pretty sure looking after one dog is going to be a piece of cake."

They went to the local pet store, with Michael driving because Gus insisted on sitting with Emily, curling up on her lap so that she was quickly covered in mud. But she clearly didn't mind.

Once they arrived at the store, Gus was well behaved enough to let the staff fuss over him while Emily picked out everything he'd need. "Let's see, we need a leash, a doggy bed, dog food, treats..."

It was a long list, and Michael was sure that if he'd pointed that out to Emily, she would have been shocked at the idea of getting so much stuff when there was still a chance that Gus might have an owner out there somewhere.

He didn't point it out, of course. Not when it was so good to see her so happy. Gus looked happy, too, wagging his tail like crazy, seeming to know just how lucky he was.

"He's going to take some cleaning up," one of the store clerks said. "You should make sure you've got lots of towels," the woman advised. "And you might want to get some of this special dog shampoo."

With the backseat of Emily's car loaded up with supplies, the two of them took Gus back to the Walker house and straight upstairs to the bathroom. The little dog definitely seemed to understand what was coming next, because he squirmed quite a bit as Emily lifted him into the bath.

"This doesn't look like it's going to be easy," Michael said with a laugh.

"How hard can it be?" Emily insisted. "Gus isn't that big."

It turned out, however, that size bore no relation to the amount of chaos—and mess—that could be created when a dirty dog met a tub full of warm water. In less than ten seconds, there was water everywhere. It spilled over the edge of the tub and splashed the walls.

It wasn't that he didn't like the water. The problem seemed to be that he thought it was a game. A really fun game in which he would splash in the water, shaking himself out in a way that only served to get Emily and Michael as wet as he was. He barked at the soap bubbles, creating a huge splash every time he tried to bite one.

In a matter of minutes, Michael, Gus, and

Emily were all more or less equally soaked. Michael's clothes were plastered to him, and it was impossible not to notice the way that Emily's clung to her.

They were pressed so close together on the side of the tub, trying to wrestle the dog into something approaching cleanliness, that Michael was aware of Emily's every movement. The small brush of her hand against his as she tried to comb out one of the tangles in Gus' fur. The way she was breathing faster thanks to the effort of fighting Gus at every turn. How she was mere inches from him as Michael held Gus in place. And how sweetly she was taking care of the dog who had come so unexpectedly into her life.

It took them a half hour to get the dog clean and dry. Thirty minutes in which they were tangled together next to the tub, trying to get Gus to stay still long enough to get him cleaned properly. A half hour in which the chemistry between them started to simmer in a *serious* way. One that Michael could tell even Emily was hard-pressed to try to ignore.

It would have been so easy to reach out and touch her just then, and Michael was almost, *almost*, certain that touch would spark into more. But he'd promised himself that he would wait until the time was right—that he wouldn't risk letting her push him away again—so he forced himself to hold back.

Finally, they were done, and Gus looked like a completely different dog. "Thank you for helping me with him," Emily said, water clinging to her face and arms. "I didn't think we'd get this wet."

"I needed to clean up after working in the garden anyway," he joked.

"Could I make you dinner as a thank-you?"

"You don't need to do anything to thank me, Emily. I was happy to help." He grinned. "But you know I'm always up for dinner."

She was laughing as she headed to her bedroom to change into something dry after giving him one of her father's shirts to put on while she put his into the washing machine. By the time Michael got both himself and the bathroom cleaned up, Emily was almost done making dinner. She'd made salmon and pasta for the two of them, and Gus got a dish of dog food on the floor close to the kitchen table.

"Gus was really nice about the bath," she said as she looked fondly at the dog wolfing down his dinner. "It went better than I thought it would."

"Fortunately, some things work out better than you think they will," Michael agreed. "I'm starting to think that sometimes you just have to take a leap of faith and go for what you want."

She stared at him for a long moment—long enough that he wondered if she was finally thinking about taking a leap of faith with *him.* But when the dog came over to let her scratch him on the head, giving a sigh of extreme pleasure at her touch, all she ended up saying was, "Gus was a very good boy. Do you want to take him for a walk with me now?"

Michael got up to take their plates to the sink. "Sure, I'll go get his leash."

With his new collar and leash and freshly cleaned fur, Gus looked really cute as they headed into town. He occasionally darted off to investigate an interesting smell, but he always came back to be as close to Emily as possible.

Michael knew exactly how Gus felt.

This moment was so nearly everything Michael had ever dreamed of. A simple life for the two of them, with their own dog, their own house. But he didn't want to be just Emily's friend who dreamed of something more with her. He wanted to actually *have* more with her. He wanted to go beyond friends. Way beyond, not only to becoming lovers, but to the point where they both knew that they were each other's *forever.*

They walked back up to the Walker house, stopping on the porch, and Emily laughed as Gus rolled onto his back, silently demanding that she scratch his tummy. "It seems that my new dog is good at asking for what he wants, isn't he?"

Yes, Michael thought, he sure was. And because Gus was good at asking, he was getting his tummy tickled. Briefly, just briefly, Michael thought about heading home—this had been a perfect day with Emily, and he didn't want to do anything to spoil it. But he couldn't leave.

Not until he took a page out of the dog's lesson book and finally asked for what he wanted, too.

"Emily?"

"Hmm?"

"I want to kiss you."

That got her attention, and he guessed that she was probably about to say something about how they couldn't, or shouldn't, kiss. But Michael couldn't bear to hear that.

And he couldn't keep his distance from her for one more second, either.

So he took another step closer, took one of her hands in his to draw her to her feet, and kissed her. Kissed her with all the love in his heart. Kissed her with all the passion that had been simmering between them all day...and for years before that.

For the first moment or two after their lips met, she went perfectly still, as if in complete shock. But then—*thank God*—she began to kiss him back. With an intensity that stunned him.

Michael could taste her mouth against his, sweet and soft and *perfect.* And as he held her close to him, they were two people who needed one another completely.

He had often dreamed about what it might be like to kiss Emily. But the reality was far more than anything he had imagined. More beautiful. More intense. Just *more.*

No other kiss he'd ever had even came close to it. And when they finally pulled back from one another, he found himself trying to catch his breath, and he could see Emily was doing the same.

He thought about kissing her again, even

more passionately this time and telling her once more about everything he felt for her. Yet Michael knew Emily too well for that. If he pushed any further, she would just push back, and probably push him away altogether. Or he could force himself to take a step back and have faith that she would face the truth of her emotions in time.

She'd always been the person he trusted most. With everything...especially his heart. So he would trust her yet again.

Which was why he simply gently pressed his lips to hers one more time before saying, "I had a great day with you, and I'm happy you found Gus," then making himself leave, while hoping that Emily would think about their kiss for the rest of the night. Just the way he knew he would.

All night long.

CHAPTER TEN

Gus looked up at Emily, apparently waiting to see what they were going to do next. The trouble was, Emily wasn't sure *what* she should do. She was still too stunned by the amazing kiss Michael had given her—two kisses actually, one incredibly passionate, one incredibly sweet—to think straight.

After Michael disappeared out of sight, she unlocked the front door and walked inside, followed closely by Gus.

She felt as if she were in a fog as she took off his leash and sat down on the sofa. He jumped up beside her. Emily knew that she probably ought to keep him off the furniture from the start if she didn't want him thinking that he owned the place. Yet, right now, she needed the company. Desperately needed it, actually.

"Michael kissed me."

Gus woofed in response.

"Yes, I know you were there, but you don't understand. He *kissed* me!"

It had felt like so much more than just a kiss. The best kiss of her life, by miles. So good that she'd been utterly swept up by it, instinctively kissing him back before she could do anything else. So good that she hadn't wanted it to end.

She was snapped out of that thought by the wetness of a tongue against her face. It seemed that Gus had decided she needed to be kissed again. At least with Gus, it didn't bring any complicated issues or feelings with it.

Because that kiss with Michael had brought plenty of feelings with it—*all* of them complicated.

Emily closed her eyes, remembering every wonderful detail of his mouth pressing against hers. The delicious taste of him. The heady feel of his muscles pressed so close to her, closer than ever before.

His strength had always comforted her, but that was when she'd been so sure of where Michael fit into her life. Now...well, she honestly didn't know where either of them fit anymore.

Gus barked again, and Emily felt the soft weight of him pressed against her leg. "I know living with me is a big change for you and that change can be scary, but don't worry, you're safe now."

Change. So much had changed, first with her sisters over the past year, and now between her and Michael.

"This time on Saturday I was just trying to make sure everything at the wedding went off without a hitch. But today everything is different and complicated."

Thinking she needed to get her mind off of things, she went to the kitchen. But what was the point of cooking when there was no one to cook for? She decided to clean up instead, but that took about five seconds since she always kept the kitchen spotless. She got out her dusters and set to work on the creaking old banister—she hadn't given it a good going-over in a while. But even that was a mistake, because she could make out the spot where Michael had replaced a couple of risers on the stairs after Hanna had damaged them as a kid.

Gus followed her everywhere she went, always standing just a little way behind her, as if he'd decided that his new role in life was to guard her against anything that might hurt her. Just the way Michael always had, she realized as her chest clenched tight.

"If he kissed me, then he can't have possibly been ready to forget about what he said Saturday, can he?" Emily asked Gus, even though he was just a dog and couldn't possibly have any answers for her. "You don't know about Saturday, do you?" she mused aloud. "Though you might have been around the old homestead since that's where we found you today. Saturday is when Michael told me that he loved me. And that he knew I loved him, too."

Gus lay down at the foot of the stairs, his head on his paws, listening intently.

"When he didn't say anything at breakfast yesterday, I figured he must have just been swept up in the wedding romance. You know, that he hadn't meant it and was too embarrassed to say anything."

Gus went on staring at her, his eyes moving back and forth as if he was trying to understand what she was saying.

"And I told myself that was a *good* thing. That I was glad he didn't say anything more about it over breakfast, or today. But..."

Emily found a spot of stained wood and set to work with the beeswax polish, not caring that it would probably take three or four coats to get anywhere close to the finish she wanted. She just needed something to keep her busy so that she didn't stew too much over Michael.

And his kisses.

And how she wished he were here right now so that she could kiss him some more.

How could his kiss pack so much meaning?

Maybe it was because thoughts of Michael brought with them all the memories of the boy who had been like a brother to her sisters growing up, the man who was always so ready to help out. And also the man who was not afraid to tell her what he felt. Who wasn't afraid to tell her that he knew she was in love with him.

"Why does life have to be so complicated? Why does everything have to keep changing?"

Gus, who had started to doze off to the soothingly repetitive sound of her rubbing the polish on, opened one eye.

As Michael had said, things would be different now that Paige wasn't here anymore. Emily knew her sister would visit, but not often enough for an allergy to Gus to be a big problem. Paige was off with Christian now, following a busy schedule that came from a combination of his film roles and her increasingly demanding choreography contracts.

It wasn't just Paige, either, although her absence was the biggest and most recent. Just a few years ago, the house had been full of Walkers. Looking back, though, it was easy to see that things had been changing around the Walker house for years. Rachel had gone off in search of a life away from the island, only to come back with a daughter in tow. Morgan had left, going to New York to pursue her career. Hanna had gone to Seattle for her studies.

But the recent changes in the past year were more permanent. More important. And even though her sisters were still connected to the island, and they all came back for holidays and family occasions, the fact was that they had scattered to the four winds.

And Emily could see that things were never going to be the same again.

"I'm not jealous," she said as she put down her polish to sit on the stairs and pat Gus' head. "I love my sisters. I'm happy for them. I want them to be happy, and I would never drag them back here. I don't want to hold them back at all, but let's face it, while you're great at listening, you can't talk things out with me the way they all can."

Gus barked pretty much on cue, but it wasn't exactly meaningful advice—and she could have done with some of that right then. The kind of advice that, on a normal day, she would have been able to get by talking to Grams. Yet she wasn't here, either.

Emily couldn't even go to her father to ask his opinion about what was happening with Michael, since he was off in Europe. The fact that she was even thinking of going to her father for advice said a lot about just how much she needed to talk to someone right then.

She'd grown up quickly, raising her sisters while her father stayed away as much as he could. Looking back, it was easy to see how angry she'd been at being left alone like that. And she'd had a right to be. But now, the one time that she could do with his advice, the one time she wanted to seek him out, where was he? In Italy, away as usual.

It was moments like this when she wished her mother were still alive. No, that wasn't true. She wished for that *every* day. But on a day like today, when Emily simply didn't know what to do, it was all too easy to imagine what her mother would have done.

Ellen Walker would have put an arm around

her oldest daughter and talked her through everything. Or maybe she would have just listened. Either way, by the time she would have been done talking, Emily was sure that the whole situation would have made perfect sense and she would have known what to do.

It was what Emily had always tried to do for her sisters.

Today, however, it looked like it was just her, Gus, and a big house that seemed far too empty without a whole family to fill it. Meanwhile, Michael's kisses still tingled on her lips as she went round and round in her head wondering what to do...

CHAPTER ELEVEN

Pulling back after kissing Emily and walking away was one of the hardest things Michael had ever done. He certainly hadn't wanted to when every instinct had been telling him to hold her closer instead...and never let her go. Yet he knew with perfect certainty that anything *but* walking away would have risked driving Emily away forever.

He'd been in love with her for so long that he understood her in ways even her own siblings might not. She would need time to adapt to the reality—and the intensity—of what they both felt for one another. Heck, after that kiss, even Michael was a little stunned by the heat and sparks they'd generated.

Fourteen years ago, he'd made his first big move toward winning her heart. And as he sat alone on his front porch and looked toward her home, his memories took him back to that day.

* * *

The Walker house, fourteen years ago...

"But why do you have to move out?" Emily asked, standing in the middle of the kitchen with the rest of her family.

"It's not like I'm going far," Michael said. "Just back to my parents' house." The house he'd inherited.

He'd always intended to move out of the Walker home after high school graduation. He was packed and organized, but that didn't mean that his move was going to be easy.

"You don't have to go, Michael," Tres said. "You're welcome here for as long as you want to stay."

Mr. Walker's offer meant a lot to Michael, but it was time he got out on his own. Not just for himself—but also because there was no way he and Emily could ever have a relationship if he was living in her house like a brother.

"I don't want you to go," Hanna said as she rushed over and wrapped both arms around his legs.

"I won't be far away." Michael gave her a big hug so that she would know how much he cared about her.

Rachel, normally so rebellious but today looking pretty subdued, took hold of Hanna's arm and gently drew her away.

"I've loved living here with all of you, but moving back into my own home is something I have to do."

"You still haven't said why," Emily pointed out.

How could he tell her his reasons in front of everyone? He loved the Walker house and everyone in it. He loved that Ava had become Grams to him as much as everyone else. He loved the way Paige was constantly finding excuses to head down to the dance studio, and Morgan's attempts at acting, and Hanna's role as the center of attention. He even loved Rachel's refusal to be pinned down by anyone else's rules and expectations, even though he knew how it worried Emily. He loved the way Mr. Walker had simply stepped up and taken him in when he'd needed it.

But Michael had fallen in love with Emily...and that had changed everything.

"I need my own space for a while," was what he finally said. "I need to work out who I am."

"You're our big brother," Morgan said. Only a little older than Hanna, she was clearly just as upset at the thought of him leaving.

Being the oldest, he and Emily had always done their best to look out for the others. She had managed to fill the hole left by the girls' mother, and he had kind of filled in for their father. They'd tried to make it one big happy family.

But that was just the problem—he wasn't their brother. And if he stayed, Emily was never going to be able to see him as anything other than one.

He'd known how he'd felt about her for a long time, but he knew he couldn't say anything when he was staying under the same roof. It would make things too complicated for both of them. For the whole family, probably.

"How are you going to make a living?" Rachel asked.

"Graham Deenes has offered to take me into his construction business. I'll concentrate on building here on the island, and that will allow him to work more on the mainland."

"So you're going to move out just like that?" Emily said.

Usually, she was good at hiding when she was hurt about something. How many times had she waited for Hanna and Morgan to be asleep before she talked to him about her worries and concerns? But today, she didn't seem to be doing a very good job of hiding any of her emotions. She clearly didn't want him to leave. And even though he hated to upset her, he hoped that was a good sign.

He wanted to reach for her, wanted to pull her close and tell her everything that was in his heart. Instead, he simply nodded in answer to her question.

"You're going to come back, aren't you?" Paige asked. She'd been pretty quiet up to then, but that was nothing new.

"As often as I can," Michael assured her, although he was looking at Emily while he said it. "I'm only a couple of blocks away. Also, I figured I could maybe come around for breakfast sometimes before I head out for the day."

"Every day," Hanna insisted. "You have to come every day."

Emily shrugged, saying, "Breakfast will work, if you want."

Her shield had finally come down, and he knew she was trying to pretend that nothing was wrong. She was trying to be the strong one, like always. It nearly killed him not to go to her, but before he could, Grams came forward and hugged him.

"Sometimes we have to leave to get everything we want," she said.

In that moment, Michael wondered if Grams had guessed all his reasons for leaving. Had she known all along just how much Emily meant to him?

Grams lowered her voice so that only he could hear her. "But that doesn't mean that you can't visit every day. You might not want to be a brother to one of my girls, but remember that you're still a brother to the rest, and we all want you here."

"I'll remember that," Michael promised, giving her a hug.

"See that you do," Grams replied. "One more thing," she added as she stepped out of his arms. "You've got all these boxes, but I think you've left the most important one upstairs."

Michael wasn't sure what Ava was talking about. Even so, he knew better than to argue with her. Grams was a force of nature holding everything and everyone together. She had given the girls happy childhoods almost by sheer force of will, making sure that they never wanted for anything. Anyone who had ever tried to question their unusual living situation had quickly found themselves faced with the full force of Ava's personality.

He headed upstairs to his room and instantly recognized the box that sat on his bed. "Emily's memory box," he said aloud as he picked it up. Small and made of wood, it was about the size of a shoebox, painted with blue and gold stripes.

They were six years old when Emily's mother had come up with the idea. *"It can be a box to put your special memories in. You should never forget all the things you dream about when you're children."*

Inside the box were pretty shells from days spent on the island's beaches. A ribbon that had gone around one of Emily's first attempts at baking a cake, which had won first prize at the island's annual fair. Over the years, Emily had continued putting things into the box, including a piece of paper that he now carefully unfolded.

It was part of a high school project in which Emily had been tasked with drawing her dream home. A lot of the kids had just put together magazine pictures of the exteriors of houses, but Emily had sat with her mother and Michael to create something that looked more like an architect's drawing containing all the things she'd wanted. A big kitchen to bake in and all the rooms laid out in an open-plan sort of way so that there was plenty of room for family.

"When I'm older, I want to live in a house just like that," Emily had declared.

"You will," Michael had promised her. "Even if I have to build it myself."

The next weekend, Ellen had died. Her illness had been so sudden. So totally devastating. Now, Michael traced his fingers over the plans, seeing the places where tears had smudged the drawing.

Destroyed by grief, Emily had ripped the drawings up. "What's the point of making plans when things don't work out? You do everything right, work hard, try to be a good person, and life still does this!"

She'd thrown the pieces across the room, and after she'd left, it had taken Michael an hour to stick them all back together. He'd put them back in her memory box and given the box to Ava for safekeeping.

Michael had known when he'd worked with Emily to draw up those plans that he wanted to build houses. He loved working with his hands, loved being outdoors...and loved feeling like anything could be put back together with enough patience.

Now, however, it felt so strange staring at the plans on the day he was moving out. The day he was about to start work on the career he'd promised himself.

He hated having to leave the Walkers like

this. He'd seen the look of betrayal in Emily's eyes when he'd announced that he needed to live at his parents' old place. She probably thought that he was abandoning her the way so many other people had. But Michael had no intention of ever doing that.

He put the house plans back into the memory box. Should he hand this to Emily? But something told him the time wasn't right yet. So he put the box in a duffel bag, collected the last few things from his room, and headed back downstairs.

Emily was the only person waiting for him by the front door. "Where is everyone?"

"They're all getting ready to help you move in, like it's some big adventure," she said, hurt still resonating in her voice.

"I'll still be around if you need me. I'm not going far."

Her eyes were such a clear, pure blue as she said, "But you are going."

Michael nodded. He would go, and he would take the memory box with him. And then, one day, when he was certain that it would make her happy more than it would upset her, he would give it back to her.

Until then, it would be a reminder of exactly why he was leaving, and exactly what he was hoping to come back to.

Love.

He wanted so badly to kiss Emily good-bye, but that was why he was leaving. Because he couldn't kiss her. Not yet. Not until she stopped looking at him as a foster brother and a friend and started seeing him as something more.

He settled for hugging her instead, breathing her in as he held her close...and wishing he never had to let her go.

"We should go," Emily said as she stepped back, out of his arms. "Hanna and Morgan were talking about decorating your house with silver sparkles. They'll probably do it if you don't keep an eye on them."

"I will. Thanks for the tip," Michael said. "Just remember, I'll be here for everyone. Especially you."

"I'm fine," Emily said, drawing herself up. "I'm always fine. I have to be."

But Michael knew the truth. Emily wasn't always fine, and right now was a perfect example. One day soon, however, he hoped he could show her that she wasn't alone. Because he would always love her and be there for her.

No matter what.

CHAPTER TWELVE

Present day, Walker Island...

First thing the next morning, even though he had a full day's work waiting for him remodeling the house of a retired businesswoman on the other side of the island, Michael drove down to Cameron's veterinary office. The waiting room was packed with animals and their owners. A couple of girls had a guinea pig in a cage, several cats were loudly complaining, one large dog was staring at the cats with obvious mistrust, and an elderly man had brought in a tortoise that seemed to be extremely irritated at having its rest interrupted by all the noise.

"Could I get in to see Cameron for a minute?" Michael asked the receptionist. "It won't take long."

She gestured to the chaos around her. "Sorry, but I don't think he's going to have a moment for at least another hour."

"I can wait." He'd just call his client and explain that he was delayed. Even if he lost the job over being late, Emily was more important than any construction project could ever be. "Could you at least tell him that I'm here? My name is Michael Bennet." When she agreed to do that much, Michael quickly made his call, then settled in for the long wait.

"Timmy's going to be fine, Mom, isn't he?" a teenage girl asked her mother as she held a kitten wrapped in a blanket on her lap.

"I'm sure he will, Savannah."

But the mom didn't sound as certain as she pretended to be, and Michael could hear the worry in the woman's voice, not just for the kitten, but for her daughter, too. The worry that if something went wrong, it would hurt her daughter.

That was why Michael needed to speak with Cameron again. They'd helped talk Emily into taking a risk when it came to taking Gus home. But now, Michael needed to make sure that the woman he loved wasn't about to end up being hurt because of that risk.

Emily might seem tough to outsiders, but Michael knew that she had a few really soft spots. Give her someone else's problem to deal with, and she would be both practical and caring. And if anyone upset one of her sisters, it was like poking a mother bear. Not to mention the fact that anyone who hurt one of the Walker sisters would also have to deal with Michael.

But there were things that hurt Emily. Deeply. He knew better than anyone just how much the loss of their mother had hurt her. He'd watched her struggle every time one of her sisters left the island, even as she encouraged them to go with a wide smile on her face.

"Michael," Cameron said, stepping out of his office as a woman left with a macaw in a cage. "Tracey said you needed to have a quick word with me? Come on through."

Cameron's office was clean and orderly in spite of the mess many of the animals must create. It was a total contrast to the places Michael usually worked, where all the plans and systems in the world couldn't stop the mess and debris from building up every time he turned around. How many times had Emily stopped him at the door to the kitchen, reminding him to take off his mud and dust covered work boots before he came in? Just like a girlfriend or wife would. Only she wasn't either of those things to him.

Not yet, anyway.

"I wasn't expecting to see you again so soon." Cameron glanced past Michael. "Is Emily with you today?"

Michael caught the hopeful note in the other man's voice. "She's busy with the garden tours and Gus."

"How are they doing together?"

"Really great. Which is why I wanted to ask, did you get a chance to make any calls to find out if Gus has been reported missing?"

"I did and also sent out some emails. No one has reported a Spaniel missing."

"What are the odds that someone is going to claim him? Because I'm pretty sure it would crush Emily if she had to give him back. You saw how much she held back from taking him in the first place, even though she loves dogs."

Cameron shook his head. "Honestly, the chances are slim to none—which I should have made more clear to her yesterday when she brought him in. We get dogs coming in off the ferry, and they're almost always abandoned. Strays no one wants anymore. People who care enough about their pets almost always chip them. Gus wasn't chipped, so…"

"We don't have to worry about it?"

"Exactly."

"Good," Michael said. It was more than good, actually. It meant that Emily wasn't going to have one more thing that mattered to her taken away. "Thanks for your help, Cameron. I appreciate it. I'd better let you get to that tortoise. I think he's getting tired of waiting."

"At least they don't run off in a hurry," Cameron joked. And then he said, "Actually, if you have another minute, there is something I wanted to talk to you about."

For a moment Michael wondered if Cameron was having problems with his building. What else would he want to talk to him about? But then it hit him—the vet's office looked in perfectly fine shape, whereas Cameron had looked at Emily with clear interest yesterday.

"It's about Emily." The other man looked a little uncomfortable, but also hopeful, as he asked, "Do you happen to know if she's single at the moment?" Before Michael could reply, he said, "I figured that if anyone knows whether Emily has something going on at the moment, it would be you. After all, you're practically like a brother to her. And if there isn't anyone else, then I was thinking that maybe you could put in a good word for me? Sound Emily out, let me know what she's thinking, so I know whether she's likely to say yes when I ask her out on a date."

They might be old friends, but Michael could feel his fists clenching automatically at the thought of the vet going anywhere near Emily. And, clearly, he didn't have much of a poker face, because in those few moments after Cameron finished speaking, the other man's eyebrows went up and he actually took a step back from Michael.

"Unless...there *is* something between you and Emily?"

Cameron looked genuinely surprised by the thought that the two of them could be together. Was it so hard to picture?

"I didn't mean to put my foot in it." Cameron raised his hands. "I won't say anything to her. I was only thinking that if there wasn't anyone else..."

"There is someone else," Michael said firmly.

"Me."

Which was why, instead of heading to his work site, he needed to go see Emily first.

CHAPTER THIRTEEN

Emily came downstairs to the sounds of barking and laughter and was glad that the house didn't seem quite as empty as it had the day before. She could hear Gus romping around and Michael saying, "Have you been a good boy for Emily?"

She'd spent all night thinking about Michael's kisses. Alternately reliving every sweet moment—and then trying to tell herself they shouldn't ever kiss again.

She should have known he'd come over for breakfast the way he always did, but she'd hoped she might have more time to try to come up with a plan to deal with the kissing. And to figure out what she was going to say to him about it.

But the truth was that she wasn't any more prepared to deal with her feelings for Michael this morning than she ever had been.

Both man and dog looked up as Emily walked

in, and the synchronization of their adorable expressions was, thankfully, enough to make her laugh despite her nerves. Gus had a squeaky rubber toy hanging halfway out of his mouth. As for Michael? Well, he just looked so happy...which made *her* happy, too.

Gus ran forward, jumping up to try to lick her face, and she cuddled him. "Good morning to you, too." She turned to Michael, "You're good with him."

"I like dogs. Always have."

When they were kids, they would meet at their spot between the two houses, then decide where they were going to go and what they were going to do. A lot of the time they'd gone to the Walker house, or into town. But just as often they'd ended up at Michael's place with his parents and their dog. It had been one of the reasons why Emily had always wanted one herself. She'd always been so fond of Jenson.

But when Michael had moved in with them, he'd had to give his dog to a friend from school because of Paige's allergies. How hard that sacrifice must have been for Michael on top of losing his parents.

"I'm so sorry you had to give Jenson away," she said in a gentle voice, knowing it must still hurt even though it had been years.

"I knew he went to a good home. And I still got to see him if I went to my friend's house. Besides, I had a whole new family to help look after. Those sisters of yours certainly managed to keep me busy."

She hadn't meant to have such a serious conversation with him this morning—especially not in the wake of their kisses, which they hadn't yet discussed. But she had to know, "Was it worth it?"

"To get a whole new family when I needed it most? To be able to stay on the island? To get to be a part of the Walker family?"

There was a lump in her throat as she nodded.

"There's hardly a day when I don't think about my mom and dad and wish they were still here, but we both know that wishing doesn't change that kind of thing."

"I do know," Emily said, the old pain of her mother's death flaring for an instant. No amount of wishing had changed things when she got sick. Things changed, people left.

And sometimes it just wasn't possible to stop either from happening. All you could do was try to figure out how to keep moving forward.

"But if it had to happen," Michael continued, "I can't think of any family I would rather have been with. And I can't think of anywhere I would rather have been than here with *you*."

Emily took a seat on the couch. She knew they needed to have *the conversation*. Sooner rather than later. Before they could fall into each other's arms and start kissing again.

"What's going on, Michael?" She made herself keep going, even though each word was harder than the next. "Saying that you love me. Kissing me. Trying to persuade me that I love you. Why are you saying and doing all of this?"

Michael moved to sit beside her. Gus sat between them, and Emily was grateful for the small, furry bolster.

"I'm saying it because it's true. I'm doing this because I love you. As long as I've known you, you've been the most special person in my life. Even when I was too small to know what loving someone meant, you were my closest friend. We always had such a strong connection to each other. And the moment I was old enough to really understand it, I knew that I loved you. It has always been you, Emily."

"But we've—"

"Done everything together. I've been with you for everything with your family. You've been with me for everything with my family. And through it all I've known that there's nowhere I would rather be than by your side."

The scary part—the *terrifying* part—was just how badly Emily wanted his *I love you* to be true. She could imagine them together so easily. She knew that they would work well together, because they had already spent so long doing just that. She wanted this. She wanted Michael.

At the same time, she couldn't stop worrying that it would change too many things, and potentially create too many problems. If they became romantic, and then things went wrong between them, everything would be destroyed.

"You're my best friend. We have so much already. Why do you want to risk messing with that, Michael?"

"Our friendship is the most important one in the world to me," Michael agreed. "But we shouldn't stay friends just because staying friends is easier. We should be prepared to reach for everything we really want...and to risk whatever it takes for something that could be so much better. So much *more.*"

Emily's head—and heart—were spinning around and around in circles as she said, "Reaching for something doesn't guarantee we'd get it. You know as well as I do that wanting something to work out doesn't mean that it will. Because if we were to go for something like this, and it didn't work out, think about how much we'd lose."

"Do you really think it wouldn't work out between us? It's not like we're two strangers contemplating a relationship. We've been all but living together for years. I'm pretty sure I know everything about you already."

"Really? Because this is a side of *you* I certainly didn't know about." Or, rather, that she hadn't wanted to acknowledge. Just as she hadn't wanted to acknowledge her own feelings for him.

Why couldn't he see the dangers like she could? Okay, so they'd shared a couple of kisses. Two wonderful, marvelous, *amazing* kisses that Emily could still remember every detail of, from the taste of Michael's lips against hers to the incredible feeling of his warm, strong body as he pressed close...

But that wasn't the point. The *point* was that even great kisses didn't guarantee that things would be okay a year from now, or two years, or ten.

Because if Emily lost Michael, then it meant she would have lost everyone. Her mother. Her sisters. Her father. And then, finally, the man who had always been her best friend.

"I've wanted to kiss you so many times, but the time was never right to try to take things further," Michael said. "I couldn't do it while I was living here with your family, because that would have made things too awkward for everyone. And then, even after I moved out, I couldn't do it while you still felt like you had to look after all your sisters. Not when we might have both felt like I was trying to take you away from them. But when I saw your sisters all finding people they love, that's when I realized you *can* be with the person you love if you're willing to go out and do something about it."

Michael reached out to take her hands, and his touch was familiar and yet strangely unfamiliar all at once. She knew his hands were rough and callused from his work, but he'd never touched her quite so deliberately, quite so carefully, before. Not even when their kisses had sent sparks flying between them.

Sparks that hadn't settled down one bit overnight.

"Michael, I—"

"Come dancing with me."

She blinked at his non sequitur. "You want to go dancing with me?"

The way he smiled at her made a flurry of butterflies start to fly around in her belly. "I've gone dancing with all of your sisters when they couldn't find another partner. Even Hanna took me to a club the moment she was old enough to get in. If you really are so certain that you're just like any of your sisters to me, then do what your sisters have done. Come dancing with me. The worst that can happen is that you'll have some friendly fun with me the way they did."

But Emily wasn't at all sure that that was the worst that could happen. As far as she was concerned, the worst—or at least the most complicated—was just how much she might want to kiss Michael again while out on the dance floor.

Even more than she wanted to kiss him right this second...

She tried to laugh it off. "I'm pretty sure that the worst that could happen involves me tripping and breaking my neck. Or breaking yours! I'm the sister who doesn't dance, remember?"

"I'm still picking you up at eight. And Emily?" He waited until she was looking into his eyes to say, "I'm hoping for the best."

"The best?" whispered from her lips before she could stop them.

He stroked her hands, and she shivered from the sweet sensuality of his touch as he leaned forward to whisper in her ear, "That maybe, just maybe, you'll start to see that this isn't a mistake."

Before her overwhelmed brain could come up with a reply, he brushed his lips across her cheek and was gone.

CHAPTER FOURTEEN

That night, Gus followed Emily into the bedroom while she started to get ready for...

For what, she didn't exactly know. It wasn't a date. Just dancing. But she still didn't know what to call it. Didn't know what to call *them.* Not after his declaration at the wedding, and then his kisses, and then the way his hands had stroked across hers and his whispered breath across her cheek had sent her heart racing and made her entire body heat up.

As soon as he'd left that morning, she and Gus had headed to Morgan's garden plot, where Gus chased birds and rabbits for several happy hours while she pulled weeds. The hard, sweaty work hadn't quite kept her mind off of Michael's kisses, or the fact that they would be going dancing together in a few hours, but it was definitely better than staying home in the empty house stewing.

It wasn't a date, and yet she still couldn't quite figure out what to wear. Emily started to look at the back of her closet, where most of her fancy stuff was stored. Not that she was dressing to impress Michael, obviously, but if she was going out dancing, then she should look good.

"I just need a dress."

So why couldn't she settle on one?

Just then, she realized that Gus was pawing at a blue dress, one that matched her eyes and flowed around her curves.

"Seriously? You give fashion advice now? You do realize that you're a dog, right?"

He barked happily, but he didn't leave the dress alone until she got it out. Gus was probably just reacting to her scent on it. That, or he'd seen her touching the dresses and was just trying to copy her. Still, Emily decided, as she tried the dress on, her dog did have good taste.

"I don't suppose you want to pick out some shoes to go with that?" Emily said with a laugh, because the idea of Gus managing to pick out shoes for her as well was...

He ran over to the closet and picked up a pair in his mouth, the way some dogs had been trained to fetch their owner's slippers. He put them down in front of Emily, looking up expectantly.

"Someone really trained you well before they lost you, didn't they?" She looked down at the shoes, heels Morgan had picked up for her that somehow managed to be sexy *and* comfortable.

"It's going to be just fine tonight, you know," she said to Gus as she adjusted her hair and matched her eye shadow to the shade of the dress. "I'm not worried about this dancing thing at all. I mean, apart from stomping all over Michael's feet, that is."

Gus gave her a look that seemed just a little too knowing for a dog. Emily did her best to ignore it.

"You'll see. I'll go out dancing with him, break his toes, and maybe by the end of it he'll see that we're just best friends. Then we'll both be able to get on with our lives the same way we were before."

Gus made a sound that was surprisingly close to a harrumph for a dog. But she wasn't going to back down as she said, "The way I see it, there's enough room for only one new man in my life right now. And you're him."

Just then, the doorbell rang. Emily looked at the clock. Had she really spent that long getting ready? It must be Michael, but why would he be ringing the doorbell? Normally, he just walked straight in.

As she slipped her feet into her heels, she steeled herself to remember that Gus was no fairy godmother picking out her dress and shoes, and Emily certainly wasn't Cinderella about to dance with Prince Charming at the ball. But as soon as she let Michael in, Gus ran straight to him—and Emily barely resisted the urge to do the same.

Michael looked incredibly handsome in dark

slacks and a blue shirt that showed off the physique he'd built up through hard work on construction sites.

"You look amazing," Michael said as he took in her dress, and makeup, and shoes. "Are you ready to head out to the club?"

No, she thought with more than a little desperation. She wasn't ready. Not when everything in her life that had once seemed so familiar, and comfortable, was now completely off-kilter.

First because of his *I love you* and then his kisses.

Instead of answering him, she said, "Be good, Gus," then picked up her small purse and locked up. Gus watched through the sidelights at the front door as the two of them got into Michael's car and set off.

"You know, to do this right, we should have walked and met halfway," Emily said. "Just like when we were kids."

Michael smiled at that. "Maybe next time."

Next time? Her heart shouldn't race at the thought of dancing with Michael more than just this one night. After all, they were just friends. So it would be no big deal...

Paige had, some years ago, declared The Warehouse, a club in the middle of town, as the best place on the island to dance. Since she was the expert on these things, it had quickly become the place where all Emily's sisters went when they wanted to put the skills they'd learned in their grandmother's studio into practice.

"Great to see you, Michael," one of the bouncers said once they'd parked and were heading toward the front door.

"Esteban, do you know Emily Walker?"

"My niece says you did a lot to help her make her decision about which college to go to," Esteban said with a smile. "Do you dance as well as your sisters?"

She shook her head. "I wish."

He looked like he didn't believe her, though, as he said, "Go straight through and enjoy yourselves."

"You know I'm not joking about not being able to dance, right?" Emily said to Michael as they walked inside. "The wedding didn't count since they were just wanting to take our pictures the whole time."

"All that matters," he said as he held out a hand to her, "is that you have fun."

Emily took his hand, letting him lead her out onto the dance floor. She did her best to remember all the lessons she'd learned from Grams and Paige over the years, tried to listen to the music, let herself feel the beat, and just go with it. But it didn't work. Even knowing what she ought to be doing didn't make it any easier to actually do it. Especially not when she was so very aware of how close she and Michael were...and how handsome and big and strong he was.

But Michael clearly refused to let her slink

away in defeat. For well over an hour, he made sure they had fun as he twirled and dipped her.

In the end, though he did all he could to keep her from stumbling, her two left feet caught up with her. When he broke out laughing, Emily found herself laughing along with him. Soon, they had to wrap their arms around one another just to hold themselves up. And every time she looked Michael in the eye, Emily just started laughing again.

"This is the most fun I've had dancing with anyone," he said when they finally decided they were too exhausted from their laughter to keep dancing. He led Emily out of the club toward his car so that they could head back to her house.

"Remember how you would never dance in high school?" Michael asked.

"With good reason," Emily pointed out.

"I would always find you outside when there was dancing, just looking up at the stars."

"You remember that?"

"Of course I remember." He put the car in park outside of her house and turned to face her. "I remember all kinds of things about you. Like how you always double knot your shoe laces. And the way you love to look for shapes in the clouds."

"I can't believe you've noticed all those things." Even the little things like how she tied her shoes.

"I love you, Emily. That's why I notice everything about you. I always have, even when we were kids."

Almost before she knew what she was doing, Emily was out of his car and running up her front walk, trying to leave Michael—and all of her conflicting thoughts and emotions and desires—behind.

"Emily, please. Don't keep running from me. From *us*."

Nearly at her front door, she spun to face him. "You keep saying that you love me. Well, what about Jessica Wokes?"

"Jessica—?"

"You dated her in high school. Not to mention Sandi, and Heather, and"—she made a little growling sound—"I can't remember all of their names. So maybe we should just call them the parade of women you've dated over the years."

"Parade of women?" Michael said, his eyebrows rising in obvious puzzlement. "What do they have to do with anything?"

"If you've really loved me forever, the way you keep claiming, then what were you doing with *them*? The way I see it, either you're lying now, or you were lying whenever you told one of them how much you cared about her. In any case I can't trust you now."

"But that..." Michael shook his head. "All of those relationships are long gone. They don't matter now."

"But they do. How many of those women do you still speak to?"

"Actually, I ran into Heather just the other day."

"Not how many of them do you say hi to if you pass them in the street," Emily insisted. "How many of them do you still *speak* to? How many of them are you close to? Everyone knows how badly all your relationships have ended in the last few years. You date a woman, and then it's like you barely even know her afterward. You'll say hi, but you go out of your way to avoid her. Is that what you want to do to us?"

"Emily, how could you possibly think that it would be like that for us?"

"Because that's how it happens for you. Can't you see it?" Everything she'd been trying to keep stuffed down deep inside was bubbling up more and more, higher and higher. "You're my closest friend. You're closer to me than my sisters. And you want to spoil that by starting us off on a path that has consistently led to you never speaking to the women you've been involved with. I don't want that, Michael. All I want..." She could feel tears about to come. "All I want is for you to please, *please*, let us go back to how we were before. Before tonight. Before the kisses. Before the wedding."

Michael stood there for several long seconds in which she couldn't read his expression, couldn't even guess at what he was feeling. Finally, he said, "Ask me for anything else, and I'll give it you. But I can't promise not to love you."

His mouth was on hers before she could breathe or blink or do anything but kiss him back. And then, just as quickly, he was saying, "I'll see you tomorrow."

And she was left standing on her front porch, wishing for all the things she knew she couldn't have.

CHAPTER FIFTEEN

Emily was an early riser. So was Michael, which meant that he had always been in the kitchen on his second cup of coffee by the time she'd come down to make breakfast for everyone.

Today, however, the kitchen was empty.

When Gus whined, she stroked her hand over his head. "I'm sorry Michael isn't here to play with you again like he did yesterday."

And she truly was sorry about Michael's absence. Because even though things had ended on such a strange note last night, that didn't mean she didn't want him here with her. Didn't he understand that their normal routine, the friendship they'd had *forever,* was exactly what she was trying to preserve? They might have had plenty of disagreements before, but none of those had ever stopped him from coming over for a meal.

She got out the doggy treats, and as she fed

Gus one, she couldn't stop remembering every moment of the night before with Michael. The way she'd repeatedly stepped on his toes. How they'd laughed so hard that they'd clung to each other.

And then, how sweet and perfect his mouth had been on hers right after he'd told her that he couldn't—that he *wouldn't*—stop loving her.

"I could call him," Emily said to Gus, who barked in what seemed to be agreement, although she knew he was probably just responding to the tone of her voice.

Then again, she thought as she picked up her phone, after the way last night ended, phoning Michael might make it seem like she'd changed her mind about them turning their friendship into something more. But she couldn't give in to that longing. She simply couldn't, no matter how much she wanted to. So she made herself put the phone down.

"Come on, Gus," Emily said after she took a spoonful of yogurt that she had no appetite for, then put the carton back into the fridge. "We have a garden tour to conduct."

When Gus whined slightly again, lifting a paw, she promised him, "Everything's going to be okay." The problem was, at this point, she wasn't completely sure that was true anymore. "Maybe he's already up at the garden. Now, come on. I bet you can find plenty of things up there to chase."

That was enough to get the dog moving out of the house and into the passenger seat of her car.

As soon as they got to the garden and she opened the door, Gus leaped out of the car, and she had to rush to keep up with him. But where was Michael? There was still no sign of him.

A short while later, a few cars pulled up next to hers in the parking lot, but Michael's truck was not among them.

Emily clipped a leash to Gus' collar. "Right now we've got guests who want a tour. I'm sure Michael will show up soon enough. After all, he told us we'd see him today, and he always keeps his promises."

Even as she said it, his promises from up on the hill at the wedding came back to her in a rush: *No matter what I have to do, or how long it takes, I promise that I'm going to prove to you that I love you. And I'm also going to prove that you feel the same way about me.*

She felt flustered as she stepped in front of the group of tourists. "Hello, I'm Emily Walker, and this is Gus."

She went through the tour on autopilot. On the previous tours she'd given, it had been enjoyable, even exciting, to teach people a little about her family's history on the island. Now, Emily found herself reliving each of Michael's kisses and every intense look he'd given her as she told the group, "Walker Island has a unique microclimate that means we hardly ever suffer the kind of storms they get on the mainland, so berries that wouldn't thrive around Seattle can thrive here."

Just the way she'd always thrived around Michael. He'd always supported her, always made her smile, always helped her with her family any way he could.

An hour later, she said, "If there are no more questions, that will conclude our tour for today. I hope you all enjoyed it and that we get a chance to see you here on Walker Island again soon."

Once everyone left, she checked her phone to see if there were any messages. Her heart fell when there were no texts or voice mails. On the way home, she stopped for groceries, but as soon as she got to the store, she realized she needed only a quart of milk and some orange juice. After all, it looked like the only person she was going to be feeding today was herself. And she didn't have much of an appetite.

When she got home and there was no sign of his truck in the driveway, she tried to shrug it off by getting out the vacuum. Cleaning always managed to distract her whenever she was worried about something.

Gus seemed to be determined to help Emily clean. He danced around the vacuum cleaner, barking, and then stole a feather duster and ran upstairs with it so that she had to chase after him to get it back. By then it was covered in enough doggy slobber to be basically unusable.

But despite all the vacuuming and Windexing and polishing, Emily couldn't shake the feeling that Michael ought to be here. Normally, by now, he would have come around asking what she was making for dinner. If Grams and her sisters had been around, they'd have been making a fuss over him the way they always did. Because they all adored him.

How could they not all adore him when he was such an amazing man?

Gus rubbed up against her legs just as her phone buzzed to indicate a text message from Michael: *Emergency at the Connor place.*

Emily's heart all but stopped as she re-read the words, then immediately texted back: *Are you okay?*

But there was no response, not even when she sent the message a second time.

A lot of things could potentially go wrong on a building site—one slip could get someone crushed, or electrocuted, or worse. Was Michael trapped somewhere, unable to get out, waiting for help?

"Come on, Gus," Emily said, her heart pounding hard with fear. "We've got to find Michael."

Please, don't let him be hurt, she thought silently, over and over again. Especially after everything she'd said to him the night before.

What if...what if she didn't get a chance to say anything more to him?

What if the last thing she said to him turned out to be how she wished he hadn't said he loved her?

Why had she been so stubborn, not just about calling him this morning, but about everything?

She broke the speed limit for her trip across the island. Walker Island wasn't particularly big, but today it felt enormous as the minutes ticked by and she didn't know whether Michael was okay or not. At least she knew where to find the Connor place, a ramshackle old building that had probably gone up around the same time as her own home, but without the same care put in over the years.

She finally pulled up outside, and when she saw the collapsed scaffolding along one side of the building, every cell in her body tightened with fear. Was Michael under there somewhere?

But just as she was racing from the car toward the building with Gus on her heels, Michael emerged from the house. He was covered in dust and dirt, but he looked okay.

Thank God.

Because how could she have gone on without him in her life?

"Emily?" He reached for her, and she swore his hands were the only things keeping her upright as she worked to get her bearings—and to get her heart beating normally again. "What are you doing all the way out here?"

"I got your message. Are you all right? You're not hurt, are you?"

"I'm fine. Why did you think—" His eyes widened with horror. "Oh God, my text. I meant that it was a *building* emergency. One of the old walls gave way and took some of the scaffolding with it. I'm going to be stuck here until late, trying to sort it out, that's all." He stroked over her cheek with one hand, very gently, as if he was afraid she might shatter. "You really thought I might be hurt?"

She stared at him, into his dark eyes. His *beautiful* eyes. "I did, and I couldn't stand the thought that what I said to you last night might be the last..."

The words got clogged in her throat, and he drew her closer. "It's okay, sweetheart." He'd never called her that before, but just then, the word *sweetheart* felt like a balm to her nearly shattered soul. "Everything's okay."

But it wasn't, and she knew she had to tell him, "I shouldn't have blown up at you last night after we went dancing. I overreacted. I keep overreacting. I was so flustered by everything, and—"

Mrs. Connor walked out just then, not only saving Emily from everything she didn't know how to put into words, but also from having to acknowledge everything she didn't know how to stop *feeling.*

"Emily Walker? Is that you?"

The last thing Emily wanted was to leave Michael's arms, but if she didn't want there to be gossip about her and Michael spread across the island by tomorrow morning, she needed to force herself to step out of them.

"It's nice to see you again, Mrs. Connor."

They caught up for a few minutes, talking about the wedding and Mrs. Connor's two granddaughters, also Emily's students at the high school, and how they were both glad that everyone on Michael's construction crew was okay.

When the woman finally went back inside, Emily said to Michael, "You have a lot of work to do. I should get going." Even though leaving him was the very last thing she wanted to do.

"I'm sorry I can't come over tonight. But I should have everything cleaned up by tomorrow night if you're free."

She couldn't keep her heart from leaping in her chest, or her pulse from racing, at the thought of another night alone with him. "Tomorrow night would be great."

When he moved closer to press his lips against hers, she was still so relieved that he hadn't been hurt in the scaffolding accident, that she told herself it was okay to let herself drink in the sweet feel of his mouth and the wonderful heat of his body.

Just this once.

CHAPTER SIXTEEN

The following evening, Michael came through the kitchen door with a bottle of wine in one hand and a box of doggy treats in the other. "Hi."

She felt shy as she smiled and said, "Hi," back. "How is work going at the Connor place?"

"Good, although if she'd called me in before the job was halfway done, I could have prevented the wall from collapsing, and it would have saved her a lot of time and money. In any case, I'd much rather be here with you than up at the work site listening to the crew swap war stories." He took the corkscrew out of the drawer and quickly opened the bottle of wine. "I hope this is still your favorite winery."

Her heart was still pounding just a little too hard simply from being alone with him as she nodded and said, "It is." No one else had ever known her so well, from her favorite wine to the way she teared up every year during the graduation ceremonies. "Thank you."

She'd let him kiss her at his job site yesterday and had justified it by telling herself that it was just from the sheer relief of knowing he was okay. But she didn't have any of those justifications tonight.

No justifications at all. Only a need, a desire, that had been growing moment to moment. Growing big enough that she wasn't sure how she was going to keep fighting it.

Or if she even wanted to anymore.

Emily had never been nervous around Michael. Not until this week when everything had started to change. And it wasn't nerves exactly that were running through her, she realized. No, it was something much closer to *anticipation.*

Still, whatever word she put on it, she couldn't stay still—and couldn't keep her mouth shut, either. "I got an email from Dad with a couple of cool photographs of everyone in Portofino. I also got a text from Hanna, who said that Grams is handling the documentary promotion like a pro. I haven't heard from Morgan, but—"

"It's only to be expected," Michael finished for her, "since it's her honeymoon."

Emily smiled. "I hope they're having an amazing time in Rio."

"I know they must be," Michael said. "Because when two people love each other as much as they do..."

The word *love* hung between them. But for

once, Emily couldn't find the words—or the will—to push it away.

And as Michael took her hand and drew her down to sit at the kitchen table beside him, she could no longer deny just how good-looking he was. Not just because of his dark hair and eyes and strong build, but because he was so comfortable in his own skin. With every boyfriend she'd had in the past, it had always felt as if there was something missing—a distance she hadn't been able to bridge, no matter how nice the guy was.

But with Michael, there was no distance.

"It's a little strange," he said, "thinking about just you and Grams being in this house." Gus barked. "I know, you're here now, too," he said, ruffling the dog's fur. "It's just that for so many years the place was packed to the rafters."

"I know what you mean," Emily said. "This house always felt so full of life to me, so cozy despite its size, thanks to the number of people in it. But now"—she paused, almost feeling disloyal for even thinking it, let alone saying the words aloud—"it feels too big." Almost as if it was a constant reminder of all the people who *weren't* there.

Michael had always been confident, always been sure of his direction. But for the first time, it struck her that he looked a little nervous as he reached into his pocket. "There's something I want to show you." The piece of paper he pulled out was old, yellowed by the years, and patched up with tape.

"Michael." She couldn't quite find her voice, or her breath. "That's the house plan you helped me with for school."

He handed her the paper, and she spread it out on the table. She'd drawn this at the kitchen table, with her mother and Michael helping her come up with ideas for a dream house.

"I tore this up, but..." She lifted her eyes to his, her heart aching for the hurt little girl she'd once been—and the wonderful boy Michael had been even then. "You saved it." She reached for his hand. "Thank you. Thank you for saving it for me."

He looked down at their linked hands, then back up at her face. "It would fit perfectly with the empty lot down the street."

She knew exactly the lot he was talking about. "That's our spot, the place we've always met each other in the middle."

"We could buy it, and start from this plan, and build a house together. We'd still be close to Ava, but the house would be *ours*."

Maybe it was crazy. Maybe this was the moment when she should have realized just how far she'd let things go—and that it was way too far. Maybe it was the glass of red wine she'd been drinking on an empty stomach that was helping to suppress the part of her that normally would protest that they shouldn't do anything that could ruin their friendship.

Or maybe, just maybe, it was finally time to admit that she was wrong to keep pushing

Michael away.

Maybe she'd been wrong about not wanting to blur the lines between friendship and love with Michael.

Maybe she'd been wrong about always putting her sisters' lives ahead of her own.

And maybe she'd been wrong about not following her heart when love had been waiting all along for her to be brave enough to grab hold of it.

The only thing she knew for sure was that it was time to reach out and, for once, take what she wanted.

She kissed *him* this time, meeting Michael's lips with a kiss that was full of all the pent-up passion and emotion that had been building inside of her for so long. So many years of holding back were let loose in a mind-blowingly wonderful moment as he kissed her back just as hungrily.

She reveled in the sweet joy of finally getting to explore the hard and rugged planes of his body with her hands, taking in the feel of him as her other senses absorbed his scent and taste and the sheer heat of him.

Emily was almost shocked when Michael pulled back, holding her at arm's length. "Are you sure about this?"

She cut him off with another kiss, one that managed to be even more passionate, and thank God, he seemed to get the message this time. They stumbled back against the kitchen table together, half-falling over it. But she wanted him so badly that she didn't care if it was in her bedroom or in the middle of the kitchen, just so long as—

They looked up at the sound of Gus barking and were both laughing—still friends even as they were about to become lovers—as she suggested, "Maybe we should go somewhere without an audience?"

Michael kissed her again before saying, "That sounds good to me." She took Michael by the hand, pausing to kiss him again halfway up the staircase, when he said, "Better than good. *Amazing.*"

And when they finally shut the bedroom door behind them, and Michael began to strip away her clothes, one sweet kiss at a time, *amazing* was only the beginning.

CHAPTER SEVENTEEN

As the sunlight came in through her bedroom window, Emily woke to the wonderful feeling of warmth and comfort. And, most of all, *happiness.* Happiness that was deeper and truer than anything she could ever remember feeling before.

She turned slightly, looking over her shoulder. Michael lay beside her, his arm wrapped around her even in sleep, as if he didn't plan on ever letting her go.

Emily smiled lazily at that thought, while the sweet, and *very* sexy, memories of the night before filtered into her morning wakefulness. Right now, there wasn't anything she wanted more than to just stay here, her head nestled against the strong expanse of Michael's chest.

Of course, that was right when Gus barked outside the bedroom door.

When Michael's eyes opened at the sound, his smile was the biggest she'd ever seen as he drew her closer. "Good morning, beautiful."

His sweet words—and the heat of his body wrapped around hers—made her feel warm all over, inside and out. She kissed him good morning, but before their kiss could turn into something more, Gus began to bark again. Louder this time.

Reluctantly, they drew apart. "Sounds like our little friend isn't going to let us sleep," she said as she went to let Gus into the bedroom. Both she and Michael gave him some love before they began to get dressed to take the dog out.

She'd worried that something like hunting around in the bedroom for their clothes and shoes would change things between them. But right now, all those changes felt perfect. Especially every time Michael moved close to kiss her again.

"What are you thinking?" Michael asked after giving her yet another amazing kiss.

"Just how good this all feels."

She didn't mind admitting it anymore, not when waking up with nothing to do but be together and look after the dog—who, for some strange reason, was barking again—was as close to perfect as she could imagine.

Gus raced downstairs with Emily and Michael close behind. That was when Emily heard someone sneezing loudly. She was halfway through the door to the kitchen when she stopped dead in her tracks, causing Michael to bump into her.

"A dog?" Paige's voice was muffled as she held her hand in front of her face like a mask. "Since when do we"—another sneeze punctuated the sentence—"have a dog here?"

It would have been bad enough if it had just been Paige. But either Emily was seeing things...or most of her family was sitting in the kitchen. Grams was there with Hanna, obviously back from their trip to the mainland. Rachel was there, too. Even their father was there. Only Morgan was missing, still off on her honeymoon.

"What are you all doing here?" Emily asked.

"Dad had to fly from Italy to bring back a really homesick student who wouldn't stop asking to come home," Hanna said, "and our last interview got canceled, so I thought I'd bring Grams..." She trailed off, looking past Emily to where Michael was standing. Her eyes widened in surprise. "Oh. My. God."

She wasn't the only one frozen in sudden shock. Paige forgot about her allergies and just stared. Rachel actually dropped the bungee cord she was holding.

It was as if everyone was taking a snapshot of Emily and Michael looking like they'd just gotten out of bed. A bed they'd obviously shared.

"No way," Rachel said.

When Michael stepped past Emily, the familiar cold dread—the dread that had so wonderfully been pushed away last night and this morning—started to pool in her stomach again. She prayed Michael wouldn't say anything, or at least that he'd say something to fix this horrible situation.

But Emily knew better than anyone that some prayers had no chance of being answered.

"It's true, what you're thinking," he told her family. "And I'm glad, really glad, that you're all here for this moment. One that's been far too long in coming."

Before Emily could process what he was saying—or what he was about to do—Michael got down on one knee.

"I wanted to wait until your family was here, Emily, because I know that family means everything to you. They mean as much to you as you do to me. I love you, and everybody here has been a part of our love story."

Even though he was right, as she looked around at her family standing in a small half circle around them and felt her heart hammering in her chest as though it was about to tear free, she couldn't let him say anything more.

This past week, despite all the ups and downs, she'd finally acknowledged to herself that the two of them were good together. That they could be happy not just as friends, but as a couple. But right now she felt as if she was on a runaway freight train, unable to feel anything but sheer terror.

On instinct, more than anything else, she pushed past her family before they could do anything to try to stop her.

* * *

Michael's first instinct was to take off after Emily. To pull her into his arms and hold her close until she understood that she didn't have to run away.

Still on one knee, he started forward, taking off like a runner out of the blocks, when Ava stepped in front of him.

"Michael. Don't."

"But, Grams—"

"What are you going to do? Run after her and tell her how much you love her? Grab her to stop her from leaving? Emily's running *precisely* because she feels smothered by it all. Go after her now, and she might never stop running."

"I just want to make sure she's all right."

"I know," Ava said. "We all want that. *I'll* go after her. And I want all of you to wait here. I might be a while. I should have had this conversation with Emily a long time ago." Ava set off, stopping only to grab some tissues.

It nearly broke Michael to resist the urge to go after her. Nothing hurt him more than knowing Emily was in pain. But Grams had been firm about it, and in his heart of hearts, he knew she was right. If he put any more pressure on Emily, he might push her all the way out of his life.

Which left him standing in the kitchen with Tres, Paige, Hanna, and Rachel. It wasn't a comfortable moment, but then, how could it be? He'd just managed to upset Emily more than anyone ever had. More than that, he'd just completely disrupted the dynamics of their family.

Tres held his gaze. "I think you and I should have a talk, Michael."

Michael followed Emily's father out of the kitchen into the sitting room. But neither of them sat as Tres said, "So...you and Emily?"

"Yes," Michael replied.

"Well," her father said slowly, "I guess we all saw that one coming. Still, I have to admit we're all a little shocked that it did."

"Please know that I never meant to hurt her—that was the very last thing I ever wanted to do. I thought I was doing the right thing, especially when I saw that all of you had arrived home. In the back of my mind, I guess I'd always imagined including everyone in your family in a moment like this. I just love her so much."

"I might not quite have my mother's genius for working these things out," her father said, "but I'm not blind, Michael. And neither are the other girls. We've all known that you're in love with Emily, and we've all hoped that one day she'd realize she's in love with you, too."

It was amazing to hear the father of the woman he'd just slept with—the same woman he'd just succeeded in upsetting so completely—speaking so calmly about the situation.

"I thought you'd be upset with me."

"Don't get me wrong," Tres said, "if it had been anyone else coming down from my daughter's bedroom, or sending her off crying, I'd be losing my mind. But the truth is that I know we wouldn't be in this position if it were anyone but you."

"I'm sorry that I—"

"No," her father said, cutting him off. "There are some things you should never apologize for. And there are some things you shouldn't ever regret, either. I loved Ellen with all my heart, and there were certainly some bad times that came after her death. I wasn't much of a father because of them. But I still don't regret one second of loving her. Do you feel that deeply about my daughter?"

"Yes," Michael said without hesitation, "I do."

Tres seemed pleased by his response—and not at all surprised. "I didn't do everything I should have for my daughters. I left you and Emily and my mother to do a lot of the things that I should have done, that I *couldn't* do. Every time I think about that, I feel so guilty about the burden that I placed on all of you. On Emily in particular. She has spent so much of her life giving to other people. Now, there's nothing more I'd like than to see her happy. And believe me, Michael, you do make her happy."

"What about all the others?" Tres' words gave him encouragement, but at the same time, he didn't want to upset Emily's sisters.

"Do you think for one moment that they would want to stand in your way? I told you before, they've hoped for a long time that the two of you would face what you've always felt for each other."

Michael was glad that he had Tres' blessing. Beyond glad. Because after everything the older man had done for him, this meant the most to him. And yet...

"All this talk of the others being happy doesn't mean anything if I've just lost Emily," Michael said.

In the last twenty-four hours they'd been the closest they had ever been, but she'd still run away from him. How could two people be together when one of them was so scared of the future that she'd rather run than face it?

"Michael, I may not have been around much, but I was still here enough to know that you don't quit. You've been willing to trust in your love for my daughter for as long as I can remember. Whatever you do," Tres said in the fiercest voice Michael had ever heard from him, "don't you dare stop trusting now."

"I couldn't, even if I wanted to," Michael promised. "I've always loved Emily. And I always will."

CHAPTER EIGHTEEN

Emily could feel the tears streaming down her face as she ran, not paying any attention to where she was going. Finally, she came to a stop, leaning against a streetlight that sat halfway between her house and...

"No," Emily said, shaking her head and wiping her cheeks roughly with the back of one hand, "I was *not* running toward Michael's house. I wasn't."

With her family staring at her like that, and with Michael doing crazy things like trying to propose to her, the home that had always felt so safe had become a place to escape from. She'd had to get away.

Gus stood on his hind legs, and she bent down so that he could lick the tears from her cheeks. "What am I going to do?"

"You could start by not running away again." Emily turned at the sound of her grandmother's voice. She had been so upset that she hadn't heard Grams approaching. "Honestly, running after you today was much harder than it was when you were a little girl."

"Grams, I'm so sorry."

"Hush now." Grams gathered Emily close. "You have nothing to apologize for."

"But Michael and I—"

"Didn't I just tell you that you have nothing to apologize for?" She said it in her *I'm your grandmother, do what you're told* voice.

Emily found herself a little surprised at just how comforting that voice was. It reminded her of times when she'd been looking after her sisters and one of them had gotten out of hand enough that Emily hadn't been able to control things. Grams had always stepped in and managed the situation. Just like she obviously intended to do right now.

"Yes, Grams," Emily said, because it was the only thing she *could* say when her grandmother sounded that certain about something.

"Now," her grandmother said, moving to Gus and stroking behind his ears, "who's this little guy?"

"His name is Gus," Emily said.

Her dog took that as his cue to roll onto his back to have his tummy tickled. Grams obliged, drawing a delighted bark from the dog.

"Where did he come from?"

"Michae—" His name got caught in her throat as all of his words of love, and all of the pleasure she'd found in his arms last night, swirled around and around inside of her. "We found him wandering around at the garden plot. At first I didn't think it would be possible to keep him."

"But Michael talked you into it," Grams guessed. "Because he knew how much you wanted a dog."

As Emily nodded, Gus moved to sit beside her, and she put a protective hand on his head between his ears. "I know that Paige has allergies, but I was hoping we could figure something out."

Grams waved that concern away. "Of course Gus can stay. Did you think I was going to ask you to get rid of him?"

Suddenly, Emily felt like a little girl again. Asking her grandmother if she could keep the dog she'd found. Running away because her sisters and father had just seen the man they'd thought of as a brother coming downstairs from Emily's bedroom.

"Everyone must be so upset with me right now." Emily sat down, there on the curb, with Gus nuzzling up against her. To her surprise, Grams sat down, too.

"Why would anyone be upset with you?"

"I slept with Michael!" Even saying the words was hard. Hard enough that she had to practically shout to get them out.

"Yes. And?"

That took Emily a little aback. She stared at her grandmother. "Why aren't you horrified?"

Grams put a warm and very comforting arm

around her. "Why do you think your sisters would be at all upset that you slept with Michael?"

Grams might as well have asked Emily why she thought the sky was blue. "Because he's like a brother to all of them." Why couldn't Grams see this? "Because it will ruin things, change things. Because if things go wrong, then they'll have to choose sides, and it will tear this whole family apart, and they'll hate me for it."

"First of all," her grandmother said in a very gentle voice, "do you seriously believe that any of your sisters could hate you?"

"They said it enough times growing up."

"That's because you were always there to do what they *needed*, even if it wasn't what they always *wanted*. So now I'm going to tell you what *you* need to hear. And, honestly, I think it is exactly what a part of you wants to hear, too." Her grandmother held her gaze, looking as serious—and as full of love—as she ever had. "Let's start with the obvious: Your sisters know all about what you and Michael feel for one another, that you love each other deeply. They have for years. They don't hate you for sleeping with him. They're *happy* for you, darling."

"But we were..."

"The two people they loved the most as children. Why wouldn't they want both of you to be happy?"

Emily swallowed hard. "They've really known for years?"

"Of course they have. It wasn't exactly hard to

spot." Grams smiled again. "Well, for most of us." She stroked her hand over Emily's back in a soothing motion as she continued with, "Tell me something. Why did you run here?"

Emily shook her head. "It wasn't...this wasn't where I was planning to end up."

"Where *were* you going then?"

"It's going to sound stupid," Emily said, because even in her head it sounded that way. Aloud, it would probably sound far worse.

"I've seen you behave in all kinds of ways over the years. I've seen you happy and sad. I've seen you trying to help people, and I've seen you when you've gone too far with that. There have been times when I've worried that you've been overprotective, or too determined to have things your way, or that you haven't wanted to take the risks you needed to in order to be happy. But I have never, ever thought of you as stupid. So why don't you try me?"

"I was..." Even with Grams pushing her, it was hard to say it. "I was running toward Michael's house. Toward him, because that's what I always do when I'm in trouble. And at the same time, I was running away from him." She sighed, a sound that seemed to come from way down deep within her soul. "Which is why I'm stuck here now in the middle, with nowhere to go."

"There are plenty of places you could have gone," Grams pointed out. "You could have gone into town. You could have gone to the school, or the beach. You could even have gotten on a ferry to Seattle and then taken a plane to...I don't know, France, or some other exotic destination."

"Instead," Emily said, "I'm here, stuck between loving Michael and running away from his love."

"So you do love him," Grams said. It wasn't a question. As she'd said before, *she* already knew the answer to that.

"Yes," Emily said, and it felt good to finally say it. To finally admit it, both to herself and the woman she respected, and loved, most in the world. "I love him, Grams. I've always loved him. I can see that now."

"But you've been telling yourself that you shouldn't love him. That you *can't* love him, because what if something goes wrong? What if you get hurt? What if he dies?"

"Grams!"

"I find," her grandmother said in the face of Emily's stunned reaction, "that one of the main benefits of getting old is that I can say pretty much anything I want to say. Besides, it needs saying. It's what you've been thinking, after all."

And, of course, Grams was right. Because just moments after admitting that she loved Michael, all the complications had come flooding back in. Her fears that loving someone wasn't enough. And that, in the wrong circumstances, loving someone would only make things worse.

"Believe it or not," Grams said, "I do understand. I lost your grandfather. And I had to watch what happened to my son after Ellen died.

What happened to all of you. When Ellen died, it shaped all of you girls in different ways. With Rachel, it made her give up caring about being safe and careful for a while, until she went too far the other way. With Morgan, it drove her away from the island. It put Paige firmly in the dance studio. Even Hanna...she barely remembers her mother, but she remembers everyone trying to shield her from the pain of her passing. And you, Emily." She pressed a kiss to her forehead. "It taught you that loving someone is dangerous. That it will hurt you."

"Doesn't it? Even if people don't leave you by choice."

"The thing you need to understand," her grandmother said, "is that it's the part where you're together that matters. I'm not saying that it doesn't rip your heart out when you lose someone you love, or when they leave. But believe me, it's better than tearing it out yourself so you won't ever risk feeling something."

"But what if—"

Grams held up a hand. "You don't get a guarantee. That's not how life—or love—works. And if it did, I'm not sure that either would mean as much."

Emily thought she could understand that. Even so, the thought of giving in to love while knowing it was the biggest risk in the world was a very difficult idea to wrap her mind around.

"If it helps," Grams said, "I truly believe that you and Michael have the closest thing to a guarantee I've seen. After all, before last night you'd already been together in every way but a romantic one since you were children. Some love affairs, some happily-ever-afters, are just meant to happen. Yes, it's terrifying at times, as if this alien part of you is going against everything that makes sense. It can feel like you're falling apart, doing crazy things. It's this strange, mad feeling. It's complicated and it's terrible and it's selfish all at once, while also somehow managing to be the very, very best thing in the world. But, most of all, it's worth it, Emily. Believe me on that. Love is always worth it."

They hugged for a few wonderful moments, a hug swamped with emotion for both of them, and then Grams stood up. "I'm going to head back to the house. You stay here and think for a while. I'll let everyone know where you are."

"You want me to stay here?"

"Right here." Grams nodded. "Unless you can think of a better place to think about that boy of yours?"

"He's not a boy, Grams."

"No," Grams agreed. "He's not. He's a fine man, just as you're a fine woman. And I'm very proud of both of you."

CHAPTER NINETEEN

As Grams walked back to the house, Emily stood up and turned to look at the empty lot behind her. Just that quickly, the memories came rushing at her.

She'd been arguing with Rachel. It was easy to do, with her sister running wild all over the island. And now Rachel had announced that she was leaving to go with Guy to the mainland. It had been an argument to end all arguments. Emily had had to walk out just to keep her cool. She'd stood right here, in the middle of the street, her hands balled into fists, because she couldn't stay in the house without telling her sister how selfish she was being.

Emily spun around when she felt Michael's touch on her shoulder. "Even if your father weren't away, he probably wouldn't be able to stop Rachel from going."

"Dad's useless." Emily's flat tone brooked no

argument.

But Michael argued anyway. "He's doing the best he can. And I don't think your mom would have been able to stop Rachel, either."

"I'm failing, Michael." He was the only person Emily could have said this to. The only one she trusted with all of her feelings, both good and bad. "I feel like I'm failing."

"You're not failing. You're doing great. But things with Rachel...it's just not an easy situation. Not for anyone."

Michael put his arms around her, then, and she finally let herself cry, knowing he would never tell anyone else that she had stopped being strong for a few moments.

This lot had been empty Emily's entire life. Now, as Gus pressed up against her leg, she did her best to see the vision that Michael had for it. Those old house plans that she'd thought were long gone had been kept safe by him for years. She tried to imagine how those rough plans could be developed into a real home on this special site.

Could they ever produce something that felt more like a home than the Walker house did?

"Walker Island is just a place," Morgan insisted, as she set her luggage at the front door, ready for the trip down to the harbor.

Emily looked her sister in the eye, determined to make one last attempt. "It's home. How could you possibly want to leave?"

"Because there's nothing here on the island for me," her sister said. "Because I'll never become famous just sitting on a lump of rock in the ocean."

"But we're your family," Emily said. "We're here for you."

"And you'll still be my family when I'm in New York." Morgan shook her head. "Why can't you understand this, Emily? Grams gets it. I'm going. That's it."

As soon as the door closed behind her sister, Michael moved to Emily's side, and she needed to know. "Why didn't you help me talk her out of it?"

Michael took her hand in his as he said, "Because people have to do the things that are in their hearts. She'll be back someday. And, in the meantime, we'll always be here, ready to welcome her back home when that day comes."

Emily walked around the empty plot, getting a feel for the trees, the slope, the views. It had been vacant for so long that it was hard to imagine it any other way. It had *always* been that way. She'd wanted to believe that things never changed on the island.

Except, when she really made herself think about it, they always did change, faster and faster all the time.

"You're going to take over Grams' dance classes?" Emily asked as Paige strolled past her on the sidewalk, needing to hear her sister say it again because she hadn't quite believed it the first time.

Paige grinned. "I already have, actually, this whole week." She looked at her watch. "I've got to get going, or I'll be late. I'll see you at dinner."

Emily watched her sister go, hurrying off down the road. She turned to Michael, who had walked up to their usual meeting point just in time to overhear the exchange of words.

"She's been working toward this for years," he said without prompting. "You know that she can dance, and dance well."

"It's just...when did Paige get old enough to start teaching classes? She's growing up, Michael, and I didn't even notice. What if her next step is to go get a part in a dance show and she leaves?"

Growing up and moving on—all her sisters would leave her one day, just as her mother had left, with grief stealing her father away, too.

Michael gently brushed her hair back from her cheek, before sliding his hand down to cover hers. "When Paige does leave, it will be for something or someone special. In the meantime, she's here with us. Maybe we should do something special for her. This is a big deal."

"You're absolutely right. Paige needs to know I'm proud of her. I'm going to make her favorite red velvet cake."

Emily smiled at the memory of Paige's stunned expression when she and Michael had presented her with the huge layer cake. She had squealed with delight and had then got on the phone and called her friends, asking them to come over to share it. Michael had been right. It had been a moment to celebrate what Paige was gaining, not mourn the fact that she was growing up.

Emily looked at the plot of land again, comparing it to what she remembered of the house plan. If they turned the house ever so slightly, every window would have a beautiful view.

Could she and Michael do something like that together—build a house and build a life together?

It would be challenging, but given how many other things she and Michael had managed to do between them over the years, maybe building a house wouldn't be that hard after all.

And maybe risking everything for love wouldn't be that hard, either.

"Thanks for helping me with my things," Hanna said.

Emily looked into the back of Michael's truck. "Are you sure you need to take everything you own to college?"

"I'm going to be away for a while, and there's no telling what I'll need, so it's better if I just take everything, right?"

Michael smiled at that. "There is a lot of stuff here, but then, you've never been one to travel light." He lifted a big box of kitchen utensils into the truck. "You're lucky Emily and I are here to help. Movers don't come cheap!"

Hanna laughed and gave them both hugs. "If I

make it to ninety, the two of you will still be here. Emily will be baking and bossing everyone around, and you'll be fixing the kitchen sink and teasing Emily to keep her laughing."

"I love you," Emily said as she hugged her sister.

"I love you, Em. And you, too, Michael." There was a mischievous glint in Hanna's eyes as she added, "I think it's fair to say that everyone here loves everyone else."

"Don't we have a ferry to catch?" Emily asked, checking her watch.

Michael nodded. "Don't worry, we'll make it."

"All aboard then," Hanna said. "Hey, did I tell you? I've been thinking of dyeing my hair..."

The fact that Emily's family had known for a long time how much she and Michael were meant to be together was a sobering thought. Had she really been putting her own thoughts and dreams and wishes on the back burner for what now felt like forever?

Michael had been there to help her with practically every big decision she'd ever had to make. He'd been there to help with everything from maintaining the Walker house, to overseeing her sisters' homework, to encouraging her when she got overwhelmed. He'd been there to help her and support her when each of her sisters had left home. With the exception of Grams and her father, Michael had been the only constant presence in her life.

He'd been by her side even when it seemed things could never go right again...

Emily leaned back against the streetlight, exhausted. After the day she'd just had, she felt entitled to a few minutes on her own. She closed her eyes for a moment, and when she opened them, Michael was there, the way he always seemed to be when she needed him.

"How are you doing?" Michael asked.

Emily shook her head. He knew how things had been since her mother's death.

"My dad's gone off on a school trip. Rachel's being impossible. Paige is always down at the dance studio. Morgan's crying about something, and Hanna's behind on a school project. I've tried to help them all, but I can't. I don't know how anymore."

"They're your sisters, not your children. You're not supposed to know how."

She felt Michael slip his hand into hers, the way he always did when she was upset, and that gave her strength and resolve.

"You don't have to do it all alone. I'm here. Your grandmother is here. You need a break. Why don't you come over to my house and I'll make you some s'mores?"

Emily smiled. Maybe a gooey sugary treat was just what she needed.

That, and Michael right here by her side. Just the way he always was when she needed him.

Emily looked at Michael's house down the street. How many hours had she spent there over the years playing with Lego blocks as kids and doing homework as teens and just talking as adults? He'd been there for her every day of her life. Just having him around made things feel better. But it wasn't only because he was always so supportive and such a good friend.

It was more than that.

Much more than that.

"I love him," Emily said, and the dog barked his support. "I know you know. I know everybody knows. I just...I guess I need to keep saying it to myself. Say it out loud. Because I've been *not* saying it for a long time. Way too long."

"Louise asked you to the prom?" Emily asked as she and Michael walked home from school together. She was doing her best to hide her disappointment.

Michael looked at her, then nodded, but it was as if he was expecting Emily to say something in response. He'd been living with them for long enough now that Emily knew when there were things he wasn't saying. Long enough, too, that Emily knew there were things she couldn't say.

Things like how she felt about him.

They'd been drifting apart ever since Michael had moved in. But that wasn't completely true. They'd been moving closer, as friends, but they'd also both been extra careful to keep their distance when they were around her sisters, so much so that they'd built up walls between them. Now, there were certain topics that they avoided, especially who they were or weren't dating.

Now, with this news about Louise, Emily worried that she was losing him even more. There was a part of her that wanted Michael to decline Louise's invitation. Because she wanted Michael to go to the prom with her instead. She wanted to ignore all the things they ought *to do for once and just do the things they* wanted *to do.*

"You don't mind me going with her, do you?" Michael asked.

Forcefully shoving down all her forbidden longings, Emily made herself shrug and say, "Mind? Why would I mind?" Even though her throat ached so much that she almost couldn't get the words out.

Had that been the start of all these years of stuffing down her true feelings? Was that when she'd first decided that she couldn't say anything about how she felt about him? Is that when she'd decided that it would hurt her sisters and her family—and herself—too much to make Michael more than just a friend?

She'd met him so long ago, but she could remember with perfect clarity the first time her mom introduced her to Michael.

"Come on, Emily, you'll enjoy yourself." Her mother was holding her hand, leading her down the front steps of the house.

"I don't want to go." She pulled out of her

mother's grip just as they got to the streetlight, but Ellen Walker didn't miss a beat as she scooped up Emily and carried her the rest of the way.

"Why don't you want to go play at the Bennets?" her mother asked. "They've got a little boy, Michael, who's exactly your age."

"Boys are silly. Can't I stay home and play with Grams?"

"Your grandmother's busy," her mom said. "Besides, you'll like Michael."

"You promise?"

"I promise. Now, why don't you walk the rest of the way?"

Emily stood with her hand in her mother's in front of the Bennets' door, waiting for someone to answer. Mrs. Bennet opened the door, smiling down at Emily.

"Hi, you must be Emily."

"She's a little shy," her mom said when Emily didn't say anything.

"No, I'm not," Emily insisted. "Boys are just silly."

Mrs. Bennet laughed at that. "Michael's in the living room. Come on in, you two."

"Michael, this is Emily," Mrs. Bennet said. "Her mother and I thought you might like to play together. I'm sure the two of you are going to be very good friends."

Michael smiled at Emily as if she was the most beautiful, wonderful thing he'd ever seen...and in that moment, she knew that there was no one else in the world that she would rather be friends with than him.

"Do you want to play?" Michael asked.

Emily reached out to take his hand, and together they ran off into the backyard, already laughing.

And all these years later, Emily could finally see that they'd already been in love with each other, right from that very first moment.

CHAPTER TWENTY

"I want to build a house with Michael," Emily said aloud, something that she now realized had always been true. "*Our* house."

Whether she'd been ready to admit it to herself, the truth was that she'd always envisioned him there with her. Something told her that her mother had known it, too.

"I want to spend the rest of my life with Michael. I want to marry him."

Now that she'd broken the dam she'd put in place so many years ago to hold back her feelings, everything she truly wanted—not what she thought she *should* want, or what she thought someone else wanted—was spilling right out. And it was so wonderfully freeing to finally be able to admit that, while she wanted her sisters around her, what she wanted most of all was Michael. She wanted something that was all *theirs*, something they created together, a family and a home. One she wanted them to build together.

And, most of all, she wanted to finally put the ghost of her mother to rest.

"I owe my father an apology," Emily said to Gus when he pushed up against her hand so that she would rub his head. "All these years, I've been angry with him because he hasn't been able to let go of Mom's memory, but..." She took a deep breath before admitting, "I'm just the same. I've been so worried about what might go wrong that I haven't let myself imagine all the wonderful things that might go right."

Of course, that could be said of all her sisters, in their own ways. After their mother's sudden death, Rachel had become rebellious and then ultra-careful, until Nicholas had shown her that it was possible to take risks safely. Paige had hidden away from the world at the dance studio, until Christian had helped her realize that she had talent and that she should follow her dreams. Morgan had run away to pursue her dream, until Brian had shown her that there were things on the island worth staying for. And Hanna hadn't known how to follow her life's path, until Joel had shared it with her.

As for her...Emily could now see that she and Michael had been heading toward this point from the moment they'd first met as children. Even though she hadn't had the words then for what she felt, she'd known he was special. They'd made an immediate connection, followed by a lifetime of being close to each other, caring about each other, and being there for each other.

At least until today.

Emily cringed as she thought of how she'd run away from him, in front of the whole family.

"I have to go back and tell him I'm sorry," she said, already turning toward the house. "I have to tell him that I love him. I have to tell him that I want to spend the rest of my life with him."

"Do you mean all of that?"

Michael was standing just a few feet away, at their special spot. And in that moment, he was a thousand memories combined into one. He was the boy she'd first met on a playdate. He was the boy who had done so much to comfort her after her mother's passing, and the one who'd been lost in the middle of the street when his own parents died. He was the man who had helped raise her sisters, who had taken them out dancing, and then who had finally taken *her* out dancing, where he'd made her laugh like no one else could. And he was the handsome, muscular, gorgeous man of her dreams in the moonlit darkness of her bedroom.

"Did you mean everything you just said?" Michael repeated, moving closer.

To anyone else, he would have sounded so strong, so confident, but Emily knew Michael better than anyone. She could hear the hint of fear in his voice and knew now that the only thing that could ever really scare Michael was the possibility that she might run away again.

"Yes," she told him. "I mean it."

To prove it, she put her arms around him and kissed him.

It didn't matter that they were in the middle of the street, or that the neighbors would probably talk about seeing Emily Walker kissing the man who had lived with her family as a boy. All that mattered was how good it felt to be in his arms—and kissing him passionately.

She wanted desperately to fit in all those years of missed kisses, but first she needed to say the words she should have said so long ago. "I love you. And I'm sorry I ran away. I was scared. Scared about how much it might hurt if I ever lost you. But I love you, Michael. Love you so much that I'm willing to take the biggest risk of my life."

"I love you, too," Michael said. And then, "Grams set me straight. She told me running after you would only make you feel more pressure. The last thing I want is for you to feel you have to run from me."

"And I'm sorry I did. I *do* want to marry you. More than anything." She turned with him to look at the empty lot. "I want us to build a house together, too, and I want to have a big family with you."

Gus' bark had her turning back toward them...only to find Michael down on one knee again.

He took her hands in his. "Emily Walker, will you marry me?"

Even though she'd already told him that she

wanted to marry him, hearing him actually say the words made her heart flutter in her chest. "*Yes.*"

Gus barked again, as if he wanted to get his *yes* in, too.

Emily and Michael kissed and laughed and then kissed some more. When they finally drew back, he said, "Are you ready to go back and give your family the good news?"

"Soon," she said as she brought her lips back to his. "After we've made up for some lost time."

All that mattered was the two of them.

Now and *forever*.

EPILOGUE

Emily and Michael stood together in the backyard of the house they had built over the last year, all their friends around them. They'd stayed true to the original design and had been continually amazed that they hadn't wanted to change a thing.

The officiant smiled at the large crowd of family and friends. "We are here today to celebrate the wedding of Emily Walker and Michael Bennet..."

Before he could say anything more, Gus bounded up the aisle, a small satin pouch tied to his collar. Everyone, including the bride and groom, broke into laughter.

"Well, it certainly looks like our surprise ring bearer is taking his role seriously."

Emily was still laughing as she looked over at her sisters, who were all standing together as her bridesmaids. They'd decided that giving Emily the wedding of her dreams was the best gift they could give their big sister, who had always organized everything for them. Any one of them could have set Gus up as the ring bearer, and she loved them all for thinking of such a great surprise.

Standing beside Michael in her long, white wedding gown, she felt her eyes tear up at the thought of what an amazing job her sisters had done. Morgan had arranged Emily's couture dress and makeup, which was extra impressive given that she had a beautiful new baby to look after. Rachel had found the most amazing caterer and florist. Hanna had auditioned a dozen different bands before she'd found the perfect one, and she was also taking care of the wedding photography, of course. Paige had turned her brilliant choreography skills loose on the complex task of getting everyone where they needed to be when they needed to be there.

"Michael, Emily"—the officiant drew her attention back to him—"would you like to say your vows?"

Michael took her hands in his, and even before he spoke, she could see every ounce of love he felt for her on his handsome face. "Emily, the first moment I saw you, I fell in love with you. I might have only been five years old," he said with a grin that made everyone laugh, "but I was old enough to know that you were, and always will be, my forever."

He broke the standard wedding rules by

reaching out to brush his fingers gently over the tears on her cheeks, and then kiss her, before slipping her mother's wedding band on her ring finger. There hadn't been one single day for the past year that Emily hadn't marveled at how lucky she was to have found true love.

"I should have known from the moment that I met you that I loved you," she said, emotion threading through every word. "But sometimes we don't see the miracle that's right there in front of us. Especially when we're scared. Only, you never gave up on me, not for one single second. You showed me that if there's a chance we might lose someone tomorrow, the best thing we can do is love them today with everything we are. I promise to love you today, Michael Bennet, and I promise to love you every day forward that I'm lucky enough to get to spend with you."

She didn't know who kissed who first, but then, that's how it had always been with them. Meeting in the middle...and being there for each other through absolutely everything, all the ups and all the downs.

"Is our wedding everything you hoped it would be?" Michael asked a little later as the party got into full swing around them.

She nodded, telling him, "I'm happier than I've ever been."

Of course, she wished her mother had been there, the same way that she guessed Michael wished his parents could have been there, too. But how could either of them be sad today when all around them joy and love abounded?

Morgan and Brian had their sweet little baby daughter with them. Emily knew they'd had a few too many late nights, but thanks to the magic of makeup, Morgan looked as perfect as ever.

"How's little Ellie doing?" Emily asked them. They'd named their baby girl after their mother, Ellen, but everyone had called her Ellie from day one.

"She's as boisterous as Hanna," Morgan said as she beamed down at her daughter, "as energetic as Paige, as rebellious as Rachel, and as inclined to think that she knows best as you."

"So, the perfect Walker?"

"That's right," Morgan agreed with a laugh. "I'm so happy for you two."

"I'm happy for all of us," Emily said as she gave her sister and new niece a big hug.

They headed over to Paige next. "Is the apartment in town working out for you and Christian?" Michael asked.

"It's perfect. I know Grams said we could stay at the house when we're back on the island, but..."

"But then it would just feel like you were visiting," Emily said.

"And I'm not visiting. Walker Island is home." She glanced over to where Christian was talking with Nicholas. "For both of us, even if we sometimes have to leave for work."

"Nicholas, Charlotte, and I feel the same way," Rachel said as she and Charlotte walked up at the end of Paige's sentence. Both Rachel and Charlotte put their arms around Emily and Michael.

"Nicholas says traveling is only fun when you know you have a home to come back to," Charlotte told them.

"And that home will always be here on the island," Rachel assured them, "even if we don't come back for a few months at a time." She smiled as she said, "Speaking of heading out again, I should find Hanna. Nicholas wants to talk to her about doing a documentary on how surfing has changed over the past three hundred years."

Hanna was currently editing footage from the sailing trip she'd taken with Joel, and Emily figured her youngest sister was probably just about ready for another project to focus on. And they all knew how much Hanna loved to work on projects that involved her family.

When Michael was pulled away for a toast with the guys from his construction crew, Emily went to sit beside Grams. "The house is going to feel a little empty now, isn't it?"

"Sometimes," her grandmother said as she reached for Emily's hand, "it seems fuller than ever, what with everyone coming back for all these lovely weddings and Morgan already asking if I can babysit little Ellie." They both looked at the precious little girl, the next generation along with Charlotte. "You know better than anyone, darling, that there are some kinds of emptiness that feel like endings, and there are others that feel like something new and exciting is beginning."

Emily squeezed her grandmother's hand. "I wanted to say—I wanted you to know—we couldn't have done this without you. Any of us."

Grams gave her a kiss on the cheek. "You and your sisters have given me joy every single day."

"Even when we were bickering and crying about boys at school and fighting over clothes?"

Her grandmother smiled. "Even then." She looked over to where Emily's father was standing. "And I'm not the only one who has loved you through thick and thin."

There would have been a time when Emily would have resisted going to her father, but now it felt so natural to walk into his open arms after giving her grandmother a kiss on her cheek.

For once, her father wasn't crying or upset at a wedding. Instead, he couldn't stop smiling as he hugged Emily tight. "I am so very proud of you, honey. I'm just thrilled that you and Michael finally worked out how happy you are together. I only wish I could have helped you two make it happen sooner."

"You took Michael in when he needed it," Emily said. "Without that, he wouldn't have stayed on the island."

There were a million other things she could have said to her father just then. But just as she'd needed to ask her father at Morgan's wedding last year if losing her mother still hurt him, today she needed to know, "If you could go back, would you still do things the same way? Even knowing how much it hurt when Mom died, would you still have married her?"

"I had the love of the most wonderful woman in the world. I have five beautiful daughters, all of whom are happy. I have two wonderful grandchildren and enough memories to last a lifetime. Of course it was worth it. Love is always worth it."

Emily looked into the crowd and saw that Michael was beckoning her out onto the dance floor. "Yes," she agreed as she kissed her father on the cheek, then went to dance with the man she loved. "Yes, it is."

~ THE END ~

ABOUT THE AUTHOR

When New York Times and USA Today bestseller Lucy Kevin released her first novel, SEATTLE GIRL, it became an instant bestseller. All of her subsequent sweet contemporary romances have been hits with readers as well, including WHEN IT'S LOVE (A Walker Island Romance, Book 3) which debuted at #1. Having been called "One of the top writers in America" by The Washington Post, she recently launched the very romantic Walker Island series.

Lucy also writes contemporary romances as Bella Andre, and her incredibly popular series about The Sullivans has produced #1 bestsellers around the world, with more than 4 million books sold so far! If not behind her computer, you can find her swimming, hiking, or laughing with her husband and two children. For a complete listing of books, as well as excerpts and contests and to connect with Lucy:

Sign up for Lucy's New Release Newsletter
http://eepurl.com/hUdKM

Follow Lucy on Twitter
http://www.twitter.com/lucykevin

Chat with Lucy on Facebook
http://www.facebook.com/pages/Lucy-Kevin/210611032291614

Visit Lucy's web site
http://www.LucyKevin.com

Email Lucy
lucykevinbooks@gmail.com

Made in the USA
Lexington, KY
11 January 2019